I0751669

the
MAKING of
DON

Krishna Gopalan

Published by
Rupa Publications India Pvt. Ltd 2013
7/16, Ansari Road, Daryaganj
New Delhi 110002

Sales centres:
Allahabad Bengaluru Chennai
Hyderabad Jaipur Kathmandu
Kolkata Mumbai

All pictures, unless otherwise mentioned, are from the personal collection of Chandra Barot.

ISBN: 978-81-291-2914-7

First impression 2013

10 9 8 7 6 5 4 3 2 1

Typeset by Jojy Philip, New Delhi

Printed at Parksons Graphics, Mumbai

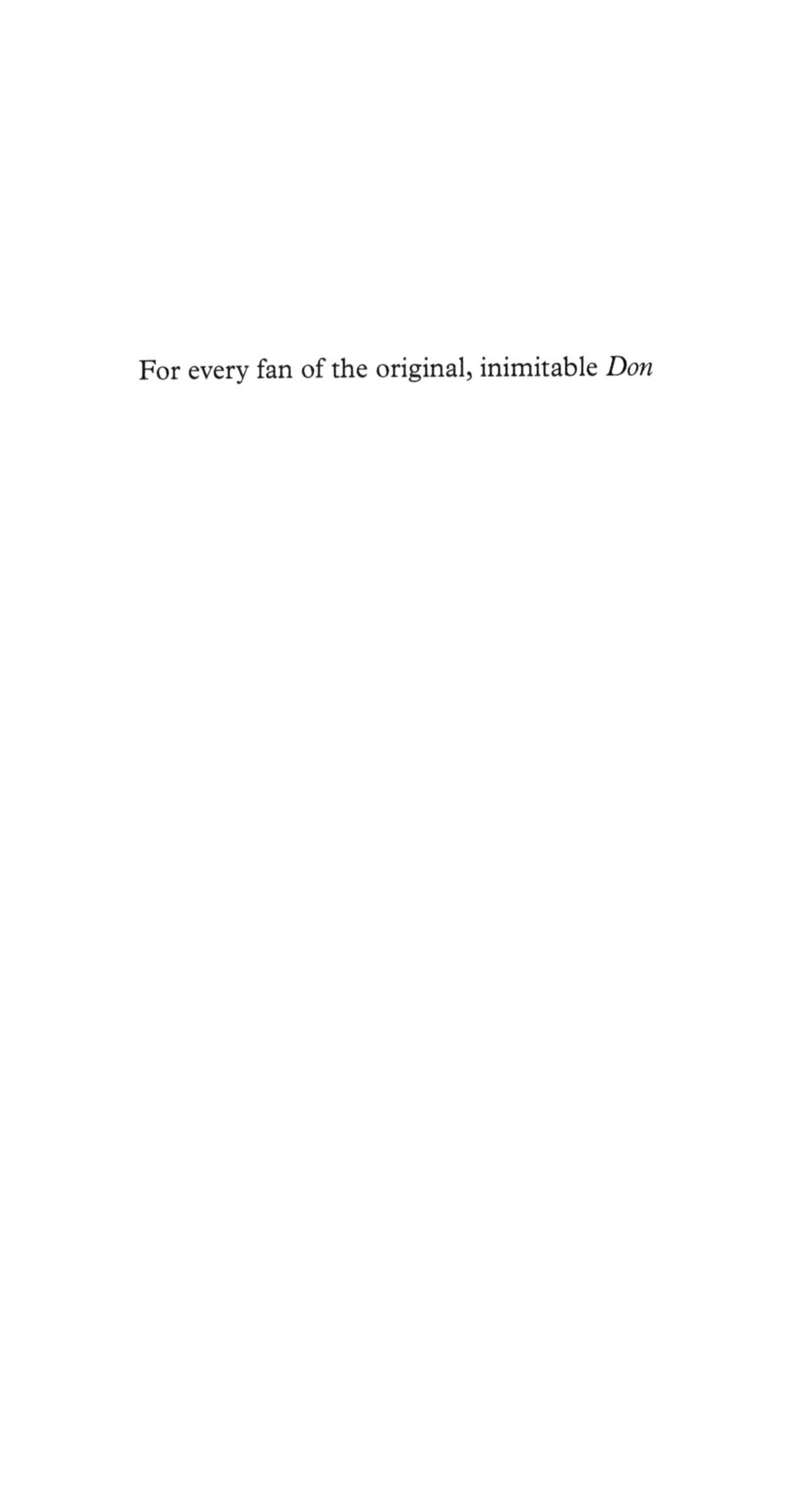

For every fan of the original, inimitable *Don*

FOREWORD

Don was not just another script or a routine project. It was the result of a thought to do something for a friend. If it is called a cult film today, the credit for that goes to a fantastic, cohesive team effort. Everyone who agreed to work on the project put aside their busy schedules to help Nariman Irani. Be it Amitabh Bachchan, the crowned king of the 1970s, who was at the peak of popularity after *Zanjeer, Deewar* and *Sholay*, or Zeenat Aman, the heart-throb of the generation, or Kalyanji–Anandji, the music directors—they all contributed wholeheartedly to the project. We were a large group of friends first and were colleagues in this fabulous industry later.

Time plays funny tricks with one's memory and incidents that were once crystal clear suddenly become hazy. It has happened to me many a time, though there is absolutely no ambiguity when I think of *Don.* I remember each day of the shooting and the joy and worries that came with it. Of course, I recall the shiver down my spine when the film was rubbished by a well-known critic. For that matter, when Sea Rock Hotel was bombed in the early 1990s, there was a sense of loneliness in my own life. I shot a good part of my film here, and in one stroke the structure was a thing of the past.

Don came into my life when I least expected it and its success was not a part of the script. I made the film over four long years, little anticipating that it would be spoken of several years later. When people refer to it as a path-breaking film, I continue to be surprised. I don't think any director makes a film with the knowledge that it will become a classic. To my mind, the noble objective is only to make a film that the audience will like. Anything beyond that is a welcome addition. *Don* was no exception to that and it does feel very good when people say it still looks slick.

I was barely thirty when I started work on *Don* and, at that age, one is nervous, confident, suspicious and excitable all at the same time. If that's not bad enough, I was in the company of people who were older than me and far more accomplished. Not once did any of them question my judgement and, in retrospect, that was probably the best thing that happened. Eventually, I made the film my way—and that was a big thing for a debutant director.

To date, I hear some really interesting things from people who have watched *Don* several times. There are those who still watch it on satellite television and ask me how the one-liners sound so fresh even today or tell me that its background music is the ringtone on their mobile. I do not know how to react to all this and it is often overwhelming. How a film with a running time of less than three hours could have such a profound effect on people, so many years later, is puzzling to me. How did Salim–Javed, a very talented duo, come up with such a tight script? By the way, I still catch bits and pieces of *Don* when it is aired and every scene brings back memories of how it was filmed or something that came in the way of it. Much of that has been presented in this book with some details that are possibly private but certainly something that the reader should know.

When Krishna reached out to me for the project, the broad understanding was that it would be the story of how the film was made. In reality, it is more about how it almost didn't get made. Scenes were shot when the actors were relatively free and songs were composed in real time. Through all this, the support of Nariman Irani made a lot of things possible. I learnt a lot from him and the film was a small way to repay that debt. Though a lot gets written about the success of *Don*, making the film, I assure you, came with its own share of stories. The reader will discover them and I think there are many incidents that even the diehard *Don* fan may not be aware of.

Farhan Akhtar came up with a unique way of storytelling when he directed his version of *Don*. It was a concept of the times that was very well received by Gen Next and it revived a lot of nostalgia for the original *Don*. I was interviewed several times and it was very satisfying to enjoy acceptance from the audience even after three decades. In the process, my 1978 release was declared a cult film and a classic. I personally like Farhan's interpretation of the film, though my own view is that a classic, as fans affectionately call *Don*, should not be touched. People like to remember the film in a certain manner and I think it is best left that way.

Don had incredibly good performances by Amitabh, Zeenat, Pran Saab, Om Shivpuri and Iftekhar, to name just a few people. Some of them are not with us any more, but their contribution to the film remains beyond measure. It is apparent to me each time I watch the film.

Don is what I have to come to be known for and I think

I was very lucky to have been a part of it. That phase in the Hindi film industry was about style and attitude. All of us were young and we just soaked in the atmosphere. It is not always a good idea to get nostalgic, but I will make an exception this time. It is not very often that something like *Don* comes into one's life. It came into mine—and life was never the same again. Yes, 1978 was a remarkable year for a lot of people. It was very special to me. It is a memory I feel very comfortable with.

Chandra Barot
October 2013

PROLOGUE

Summers in Mumbai are hot, humid and difficult. Temperatures soar well into the high 30s and often flirt quite easily with the 40s too. If the humidity level is high, it induces a sense of lethargy without any effort.

On one such sultry Sunday afternoon in 1974, as Chandra Barot eased into his cane chair, the phone rang. He gave himself a moment to wonder who could be calling at this siesta hour. It was the familiar and fond voice of Jaya Bachchan at the other end, who wanted to know what Chandra had planned for the evening. 'Nothing specific,' he said as he waited for Jaya to say something. 'Amit and I were thinking of watching *Naya Din Nai Raat*. Why don't you join us?' she asked.

In less than half an hour, Chandra emerged from his upmarket Peddar Road apartment and took the drive to Andheri to meet the Bachchan couple at the landmark theatre complex—Amber, Oscar and Minor. It had been a while since *Naya Din Nai Raat* had released. The feedback on the film was positive and everyone was effusive about Sanjeev Kumar's performance. Jaya, as the girl who runs away from home to escape getting married, was also impressive. Sanjeev played nine remarkably different roles in the film.

The show that evening was for a select gathering. Chandra and the Bachchans were quickly engrossed in the film and kept hearing the audience gushing about Sanjeev. 'This man is so versatile,' was what they heard throughout the film.

An hour and a half into the film and Jaya had already encountered Sanjeev in six roles that ranged from a wealthy widower, a drunken lout in a brothel to a psychiatrist. If these six characters were serious yet witty, it was the seventh that caught Chandra's attention. This was Sanjeev as a transvestite stage artist running a troupe called Fulkunvar Theatrical Company.

Dressed in a spotless white kurta and dhoti, this character was never to be seen without the betel nut or the paan stained lips. The audience was in splits as it saw and heard the slightly effeminate Sanjeev at his best. In the film, he asks Jaya to be the leading lady in his play. The lady grudgingly agrees to help him.

As Chandra saw Sanjeev with the paan, his mind was already working furiously. 'Tiger, this is your character in our film. Take a good look at Sanjeev here,' he whispered into Amitabh Bachchan's ears. The tall actor smiled and did not say anything. He just observed the character for every minute detail.

As everyone went home after an evening of entertainment, Chandra's mind was still ticking. It was imperative for him to build on the Fulkunvar character. He was intuitively convinced that he had hit a goldmine; now the job on hand was to give that character a certain form and shape. In a few weeks, he was ready to describe the character in complete detail to Amitabh.

Film-making is often the art of serendipity. Fulkunvar was an accidental discovery and no one would have anticipated that the emergence of a character from that transvestite would captivate the nation's imagination in about four years. Neither Chandra nor Amitabh had the faintest inkling of what was to follow. A project called *Don* was still a long way from completion and there was a lot to deal with at this moment. For now, the idea was just to make a film with a little money.

In a little over three decades since *Don* released, the film has acquired a cult status. Its dialogues are constantly mouthed by its innumerable fans. The film has become so popular that it has had a remake and a sequel with the star of the day. That would certainly be some kind of a first in the Hindi film industry.

A lot has changed since the film was released in 1978. Amitabh had already grown in confidence after tasting success with *Zanjeer, Namak Haraam* and *Abhimaan.* As *Don* was being made, *Deewar* and *Sholay* were released and his journey to the dizzy heights of superstardom was clearly underway. Incidentally, Amber, Oscar and Minor, over time, has made way for Shoppers Stop.

Don is not just the story of how a bunch of close friends decided to make a film for a good cause. Nor is it about how it aided Amitabh's rise to superstardom. It is the story of simple film-making at its best and giving the audience something to cheer about as they watch the characters on the big screen. It is about having great music and earthy dialogues. Quite simply, it epitomizes the art of making good cinema at a certain point in time. It is just that it has stood the test of time without much ado.

CHAPTER ONE

Sitting on the sets of *Roti, Kapada Aur Makaan* at Filmistan Studios, Manoj Kumar was deeply engrossed in his work. This was early 1974 and the film was still a few months from release. Manoj's mind was occupied with the loose ends that had to be tied up. He was so lost that he neither noticed that Nariman Irani had walked in nor did he catch the harried look on his face.

Nariman looked out of sorts and this was very unlike the jovial Parsi. He quickly went across to his protégé, Chandra Barot, and asked him for ₹300. Once he got the money, he was a little relaxed. This was the first time Nariman had asked Chandra for money. If Chandra, who was one of Manoj's assistant directors, was surprised, he did not show it.

Not too many days later, Nariman was distraught again. 'Can you lend me ₹10,000? I need it a little urgently,' he said to Chandra and promised to return the money in a fortnight. Chandra quickly had a word with Kalyanji, the musician, who grudgingly gave him the amount with a warning. 'You will never get the money back,' he said. A day before the fortnight was done, Nariman kept his word and Kalyanji was startled.

Chandra asked the cameraman what the problem was and Nariman was close to breaking down. His home production *Zindagi Zindagi* had bombed. The film that starred Sunil Dutt and Waheeda Rehman had been directed by Tapan Sinha. 'I have lost ₹12 lakh and it has become impossible to deal with the creditors. These people land up early in the morning with the milkman and I just don't know what to do,' confessed Nariman. It was just over a year since the film had released and there appeared to be no light at the end of a very dark tunnel.

As Chandra watched Nariman pour his woes out, his mind was clear. The only way to extricate the man from this mess was for him to produce another film. 'Yes, but who will agree to work with me?' asked Nariman. It was a question that Chandra had expected and the answer was spontaneous. 'We have Amitabh, Zeenat and Kalyanji–Anandji. I think we should just go for it,' he said. Moreover, Amitabh and Zeenat Aman were working with Manoj on *Roti, Kapada Aur Makaan*. Nariman looked a little hopeful when he heard this and managed to smile briefly. What Chandra had not told him was that there was a reasonably good chance of the Salim–Javed duo working for them. The writers were still the new kids on the block and, with *Zanjeer,* they had been noticed. Besides, they had already worked on *Yaaadon Ki Baaraat, Seeta Aur Geeta* and *Andaaz.*

Over the last few years, Chandra had learnt to operate the camera from Nariman and treated him like a guru. Chandra addressed Nariman as 'bawa' (an obvious reference to the fact that he was a Parsi) and the elder called the younger man 'bachu'. It was a relationship that thrived on respect and affection. To watch Nariman suffer like this was not easy and Chandra decided it was payback time.

Others in the industry who knew Nariman, viewed him with a lot of regard. To them, he was just a fine gentleman who knew his craft and went about his work efficiently and quietly. It was precisely this kind of support that Chandra was backing on.

If the actors and the music duo were in place, the rest of the jigsaw puzzle was not hard to get together. Or so Chandra thought when he reached out to Waheeda Rehman. The lady lived close to Salim Khan's Galaxy Apartments in Bandra and volunteered to speak to the writer. When Nariman and Chandra met Salim–Javed, they said that they had a ready script already. 'We have called it *Don* and we must tell you that it has been rejected by every director in town,' they confessed. Chandra did not really hear the second part of that sentence and just asked for the script. By then, the script was already being referred to, somewhat condescendingly, as the *Don* wallah script.

The confidence that Chandra had when it came to getting the basic star cast together was from his personal relationships with those like Amitabh and Zeenat. They were all part of a larger group that included others like Danny Denzongpa, Parveen Babi, Gautam Berry, Ajitabh Bachchan, Ramola and Jaya Bachchan. Here were a bunch of youngsters who just liked hanging out together. Starting 1972 and for many years after that, this motley group would often be seen at Blow Up, the discotheque at the Taj Mahal Hotel. This was the time when Bombay (as it was known then) had just two

Jaya Bachchan, Chandra Barot and Amitabh Bachchan at the silver jubilee party for *Deewar* at Taj Mahal Hotel in Mumbai (late 1975)

five star hotels—Taj and a newer property called the Oberoi Sheraton. Other folks who joined in occasionally were Javed Akhtar and Honey Irani.

The agenda was simple. Lots of dancing and food till 2.30 a.m. The party then continued at Kalyanji's music hall on Peddar Road. The musician was known for his hospitality and his brilliant sense of humour. These sessions would last till almost sunrise before it was time to disperse. Understandably, meetings like this on a regular basis brought people in tremendous proximity with one another. It was simply an instance of people who came from the same professional background who enjoyed the company of each other. In most cases, these relationships were to last a lifetime. Interestingly, most of these names would make more than a little contribution to the success of *Don*.

Chandra wanted to help Nariman, but he had not imagined directing the film. It was Nariman who spoke to Manoj and asked him for his opinion. Manoj was clear that Chandra was fully trained and competent to handle the direction on his own. Nariman respected Manoj's opinion and just went with it. Chandra, who was a little over thirty, had very little to say in this decision-making process. This was going to be his baptism by fire.

At this point the cameraman, who was still not breathing easy, told Chandra that S.D. Burman wanted to compose the music for the film. This was a delicate situation since Kalyanji–Anandji had already agreed to work on it. Nariman and his protégé decided to meet Burman to try and sort out the issue.

The following morning, they drove down to Jet Apartments on Bandra's Linking Road where Burman had a large and tastefully done up home. It was time to narrate the script and Burman was all ears. Within industry circles, he had a reputation for not just possessing a great ear for music but deciding if he could indeed do justice to the soundtrack of a film. The moment he realized it was a theme with a James Bond touch, he backed off. 'Meet Pancham for this. I am not interested,' he said as he waved Nariman and Chandra off. As the two stepped out of his apartment, the relief was palpable. Another roadblock was out of the way.

For now, most things were in place. The hero, heroine, music director, producer, director, cameraman and a script to work with were all there. The rest of the star cast would soon follow. *Don* was the name of this project and it was now time to take a look at finances and decide on when to start work.

To Nariman, *Don* was just a breakfast film. Not too much of a compliment by any stretch of the imagination and this was just an uneasy indicator of what the veteran cameraman was up against. As word of the project spread, the feedback was disturbing and uniform. It was about a flop producer and an unknown director who had got together to make a film. Jokes were all over the place on how Nariman was producing a film to get himself out of an earlier failed production. Luckily, it ended there since not too many people gave this project even an outside chance.

What, however, grabbed the attention of most people was the perceived chemistry between Chandra and Nariman. On the face of it, they could not have been more different. At a feather-touch weight of 48 kg, Chandra was quite different from the six foot frame of Nariman who was bulky and loved his paan. Chandra was a young man and spent his formative years in Africa where he learned to dress well. His English was impressive and the man fancied himself not just for his style but his easy demeanour as well. If unlike poles attract, this was a great example.

Nariman had spent over two decades in the industry and was already involved in prominent films like *Chaudhvin Ka Chand* and *Phool Aur Patthar*. The truth is he hit it off with Barot from the time they met on the set of Manoj's *Shor*. Chandra was one among Manoj's nine assistant directors. All of them were self-taught and made their name and fortune under Manoj's tutelage. They were all a competent bunch and gelled easily as a team.

In the world of films, there is a wonderful rapport between the director and the camera. Every time a director walks on to the set, he spends a second to locate the camera

Manoj Kumar and Chandra enjoying a cup of tea in the mid-1970s

and moves towards it. Manoj was no exception to that and Chandra was aware of this. He was rarely away from the camera during those critical moments and Nariman found this amusing. He just took to the young man easily and that was it.

Chandra was happy being Manoj's trusted aide, and had no complaints. It was a good work atmosphere and offered a great platform. Chandra harboured ambitions of directing a film and the plan was that his debut would be *Kranti,* which was already being discussed as *Roti, Kapada Aur Makaan* was nearing completion. Nariman's precarious financial position after *Zindagi Zindagi* altered the script and Chandra was in the hot seat far sooner than he had imagined. Eventually, *Kranti* was released in 1981.

The moment the key actors in *Don* were finalized, the

focus shifted towards the rest of the cast. If Chandra could be adventurous with his directorial debut, he often had to rely on Nariman's judgment and counsel. The young man just allowed his producer to decide and chipped in with his suggestions when he thought it was necessary.

One such contribution from Nariman was Om Shivpuri. This National School of Drama graduate was in his mid-40s and had been noticed for his roles in *Koshish* and *Namak Haraam.* His performance as Amitabh's father in the latter was not an easy one and critics were impressed. A late starter in films, Om had made his mark in theatre and his group *Dishantar* was already very well known in Delhi. The background in theatre gave him a flawless style of dialogue delivery. From Nariman's perspective, the role of the smuggler posing as an Interpol officer was complex and required a certain level of finesse. Om, as Nariman saw it, was the man best suited to play that.

The role of the inspector was the easiest one to fill. Iftekhar had played the cop in *Teesri Manzil, Ittefaq, The Train* and *Hare Rama Hare Krishna.* He had already acted with Amitabh in *Zanjeer* and there was no better actor for the role. Both Nariman and Chandra were relieved that there was no money to be spent on Iftekhar's outfits. It was rumoured that he had at least thirty police inspector uniforms in his personal wardrobe!

Satyen Kappu was the perfect accompaniment to Iftekhar. He was a versatile actor and Chandra had liked him in Narender Bedi's *Jawani Diwani.* Satyen would soon be seen in *Sholay* playing Sanjeev Kumar's servant. Another easy choice was Shetty, who was quite simply, the fighter of the day bearing a strange and yet an amusing resemblance to Telly Savalas. Nariman and Chandra were convinced that

Shetty would live his part. The buzz in the industry was that Shetty had based his look on Savalas in *Kojak*, an American television series that went on air in the early 1970s.

Pran (or *And Pran* as his screen title would state) was again from Manoj's camp and was quite outstanding in *Upkar* and *Purab Aur Paschim*. Both these Manoj-directed films were huge commercial successes. Pran had already spent over three decades in the film industry and was rarely caught repeating a performance. Be it *Jish Desh Mein Ganga Behti Hai* or *Ram Aur Shyam*, he stood out as the villain. He was subtle in *Parichay* and unforgettable in *Zanjeer*. Like most bad men, he was the quintessential gentleman off the camera.

Both Chandra and Nariman owed a great deal to the Manoj camp when it came to deciding who would star in *Don*. Often, getting the lead pair is the most difficult and both Amitabh and Zeenat were more than willing to be a part of this project. They had key roles in *Roti, Kapada Aur Makaan* and were quite comfortable with Nariman and Chandra. To them, it was just an extension of that rapport.

Likewise, Kalyanji–Anandji were happy to be a part of this project. They had already composed the music for blockbusters like *Upkar* and *Purab Aur Paschim*. If Chandra visualized the Bond-like look in *Don*, he was convinced that the duo were the best equipped to handle this project. Again, it was just getting the project off the ground that was important. Chandra and Nariman were just working with people they knew and were comfortable with. How the film would fare at the box-office was still a distant thought in their minds which were already cluttered with more immediate things like funding. In a few days, both Chandra and Nariman would be shooting the first sequence of *Don*. Another crisis was just beginning to lurk around the corner.

CHAPTER TWO

One of the biggest dilemmas that any director faces is to decide which scene to shoot first. A film is rarely shot in the sequence in which the audience sees it. For a director, it really comes down to what he thinks is right and what will help in setting a certain pace for the shooting.

There were a couple of factors that Chandra weighed before deciding to commence shooting the film with a song. This line of thinking was not without reason. The first day of filming is a nervous affair as the star cast, the director and the rest of the crew need to get used to each other. Even if they have worked with one another in the past, a new project requires a certain level of adjustment. A regular scene requires memorizing dialogues from the reams of paper that come with that. Besides, a song, if catchy, was certain to give the much needed publicity to a film.

Chandra was clear that a song was the best way to create a perfect, relaxed ambience. With music playing in the background, the actors just needed to enact their part. It was what he often termed the 'zero-tension atmosphere'.

The question was which song to roll with. After some

thinking, he decided to first shoot 'Yeh Mera Dil'. The reason for this was that it had Helen, for whom a song was nothing more than child's play. She had excelled in numbers like 'O Haseena Zulfonwaali' from *Teesri Manzil* and 'Piya Tu Ab to Aaja' from *Caravan*. Besides, Amitabh did not have to dance in the song. The actor's dancing prowess was still not a talking point in the Hindi film industry. Funnily enough, it would be all the other songs in *Don* which, over time, gave Amitabh his own dancing style. That, in a few years, would be a rage in the film industry.

'Yeh Mera Dil' was scheduled to be shot in Mehboob Studios in Bandra, a prominent suburb in Mumbai. If Chandra had a couple of butterflies in his stomach, he concealed them with some difficulty. Helen and Amitabh were quintessential professionals and that made things easy for him. What had to be remembered while the filming of this song was that it was not a romantic number. Although it sounded like that with Asha Bhosle's dulcet voice, the reason for the song in the film was quite different. If Chandra thought linking the song to the film was under control, he was woefully off the mark.

In the film, Helen seeks revenge from Amitabh for having killed her fiancé. The song is the filler between Amitabh getting ready to leave and the police coming in to grab him. It revolves around a slightly suspicious Amitabh who decides to settle with a drink and watch this lady gyrate to pulsating music. The thought of the police being moments away is far from his mind.

The choreographer was P.L. Raj who knew his craft. He had worked in films like *Teesri Manzil* (Helen had really made a mark here), *Gumnaam* and *Junglee*. He was a man who loved to play with the zoom lens. With the drink being some kind of a focal point in the song, Chandra thought it was only logical to get Helen to move around quickly holding the bottle. With the racy music and a heavy rhythmic beat, this seemed like a great idea. Not to Raj though.

The moment Raj heard about this, he was quite livid. To him, Helen holding the bottle and dancing was unacceptable. Young Chandra was in no mood to relent and Raj was not being flexible either. Diplomacy saved the day as both gentlemen decided to shoot the song their ways. Chandra finally won the debate and peace was restored. In fact, Raj loved what he saw.

By the time *Don* was in the making, Raj was a thirty-year veteran in the film industry having worked with stars like Dev Anand and Shammi Kapoor. To accept a point of view from a young debut director was merely an indication of the man's maturity. Over the next few years, Raj would work in films like *Saagar* and *Sargam*. By the time he passed away in 2002, Raj had been associated with more than a thousand films in at least four languages. A year before his death, Raj was honoured with the Dadasaheb Phalke award for technical excellence. His son, Leslie Lewis, is today a name in the music-composing business apart from being a part of the band 'Colonial Cousins'.

At a pure gut level, Chandra knew he had a winner when he saw 'Yeh Mera Dil'. He silently thanked Manoj and knew the song would not have looked so good had his mentor not rapped his knuckles.

When Kalyanji–Anandji came with the song, it sounded very good. Chandra had his mind set on things like where the song would be filmed and when he would start work on it. He then decided to get Manoj to listen to it. The following morning, Chandra was at Manoj's Juhu bungalow, 'Tulsi', and proudly played the song.

A pensive Manoj heard the song quietly and allowed himself a gentle smile. His protégé was directing his debut film and Manoj's opinion was critical. 'It sounds very good, Chandra, storyline *kya hai?* What is the storyline?' was all Manoj said. At that moment, the director wished the ground under him had given way. He just had a blank expression on his face. The song was to be filmed the next morning and Chandra had to get to work.

'I have no screenplay,' was all the young director repeated to himself for several hours. He did not get a wink of sleep that night till things were clear in his head. By the time the sun woke him up, the screenplay was etched clearly in his mind. Amitabh's gun had to be emptied by Helen and the

Helen, Chandra and P.L. Raj during the filming of 'Yeh Mera Dil'

bullets would be thrown under the bed. Chandra owed the idea of having the song integrated into the film to Manoj.

The filming of 'Yeh Mera Dil' had to be perfect since it was the first song in the film. Besides, it led to a tense situation where Amitabh would escape from the police with Helen's help and an empty revolver! As far as the audience was concerned, they would hear brilliant one-liners like *Neeche tumhari aunty bahut se uncles ko lekar aayee hai* (Downstairs, your aunty has brought in a lot of uncles) or the immortal *Don ko pakadna mushkil hi nahin, namumkin hai* (It is not only difficult but impossible to catch hold of Don).

The first shooting schedule of *Don* taught Chandra a difficult lesson. Money was going to be in short supply and every source of finance would have to be tapped. That was necessary if this film had to see the light of day. What was

Kamal Barot with Nariman Irani

not anticipated, however, was how soon money would be required. In fact, the need arose for the first schedule itself.

By his own estimation, Chandra needed a little over ₹40,000 for the 'Yeh Mera Dil' sequence. This was a lot of money for a man who lived comfortably on a few hundred each month. His producer,who was seriously in debt, was not of much help either. It was Chandra's sister, Kamal, who wrote out a cheque for ₹45,000 without any hesitation. The fact that she was from the film industry only made matters simpler for Chandra. Kamal was already a well-known singer having lent her voice in films like *Parasmani, Johar-Mehmood in Goa, Dulha Dulhan, Phool Bane Angaare* and *Gharaana.* This was her baby brother's project and she knew what it meant to him. Having been in the film industry, she was only too familiar with the ups and downs of it. One big hit was all that was needed to correct this troubled situation. She was certainly right on that one. What she definitely did not expect was how much her brother and the star cast would struggle to get the film released. In fact, getting the ₹45,000 for the first schedule was among the easiest things to do.

CHAPTER THREE

There is a certain sense of emotion that has been lost in modern-day film-making. Arguably, that is the result of more professionalism and intricate detailing for every transaction. That is indeed a far cry from the time when a person's word was worth more than anything else. Not everything had to be put down on paper and the element of trust was more than enough.

Don was no exception and the agreement between the producer and his director was standing proof of that. Chandra's arrangement with Nariman was simple and, in today's context, could well be termed bizarre. Once the director had brought in ₹45,000 for the first schedule of shooting, it was clear that the project was well and truly under way. It depended on how quickly the funds could be put together.

It was at one such casual meeting when Chandra and Nariman attempted to draw the financial contours of the deal between them. Chandra was drawing a salary of ₹3,000 each month from his already stretched producer. That was not big money, given that the young man was the director, but it was not loose change for Nariman in his current situation. The problem was that Nariman was finding it difficult to make Chandra a concrete offer as director's fee. He did make a reasonable attempt.

If the film was a hit, Nariman would give Chandra a two bedroom apartment in Bandra. Chandra was straight and candid. 'Bawa, I already have a large flat with two bedrooms on Peddar Road. Instead, you give me a three bedroom apartment and I will just pay the difference,' he said. That sounded like a fair deal and Nariman agreed instantly. The two gentlemen exchanged a smile and nothing that transpired that afternoon was ever recorded on paper. It was a conversation between two individuals who loved and respected each other. Putting it on paper or documenting it in any form would be unfair to both. One of the most important transactions for a landmark film was concluded casually over a cup of tea

Nariman and Chandra on the sets of *Don*

with no witness. It was something that Chandra would rue for years to come.

Even if Chandra saw the financial crisis befalling the film at every stage, he never allowed that to come in the way of his enthusiasm. Using his personal finances and by reaching out to every possible acquaintance, he managed to organize ₹3.5 lakh. In that scenario, it was a lot of handy money. That money was treated as a loan and a substantial 2 per cent interest per month would be paid to Chandra. That would be the responsibility of Nariman's production assistant, Chander. The interest worked out to ₹7,000 each month and that, with a salary of ₹3,000, gave Chandra ₹10,000 each month. If the interest on the loan was a commitment, there was no surety about the principal. Initially, the ₹10,000 came Chandra's way without too much of a problem. That was not to be the story later as money was clearly in short supply. Again, the thought was only about that particular moment. Tomorrow would come later.

There were other things that had to be addressed as well. Rajendra Kumar had heard of the *Don* project and was keen on participating in it. The worrisome part was that he wanted Iftekhar's role. It was not going to be easy to wriggle out of that one. It was with that thought in mind that Salim Khan and Chandra decided to meet Rajendra.

Jubilee Kumar, as he was known, was well past his prime. He may have ruled the box-office in the 1960s with Shammi Kapoor, Shammi's brother Raj Kapoor and Dev Anand as worthy competitors, but this was quite a different era. The continuous success that Rajendra had encountered with superhits like *Arzoo*, *Sangam*, *Dil Ek Mandir* and *Mere Mehboob* gave him the feeling that his current lack of favour with the audience was a temporary phase. The arrival of a freckle faced Rajesh Khanna put most of the stars from the 1960s out of business. Rajendra's eyeing the role of the inspector was obviously an attempt to restore the much estranged rapport with his audience.

Sitting with Rajendra was an unforgettable experience for Salim and Chandra. It was clear that the man had decided how his role would shape up in the film. At one point in this critical conversation, Rajendra came up with what he thought was a brilliant idea. 'Salim miyan, I have this thought for a scene and I think you should include it in the film,' he said as the director and story writer listened. 'When the inspector is killed in the film, you guys should have his statue outside the police station. Amitabh garlanding that statue will be a fantastic shot,' he added. There was a moment of silence in the room as Salim and Chandra looked at each other nervously.

As the duo stepped out of Rajendra's palatial bungalow in Bandra, Salim was the first to break the silence. 'Chandra, *yeh to jamega nahin*, this won't work...' was all he said. The job now was to tell Rajendra that it would be difficult to slot him in the film. It still remains unclear who broke the news to him and in what manner. It did not matter very much.

This was not the only kind of problem that Chandra was dealing with. He got a call from Manoj Kumar one morning. 'I believe your film is going to be called 'Down'. This is what my driver, Rahim, has read in the Urdu papers. Have you lost your mind? It sounds terrible,' he said. Chandra was aghast and told Manoj it was *Don*. There was a bored yawn at the other end before a suggestion came. Manoj thought the film would sound better if it were called Mr Don. 'Shashi

(Kapoor) has had a film called *Mr Romeo.* Your film should sound like that,' he went on to say. Chandra listened without saying much. His mind was made up. *Don* it was. Even if the initial idea was to have *Don* as a working title, it was no longer just that. Apart from sounding somewhat anglicized, there was a marketing rationale for a title like that.

Through the 1960s, and a good part of the 70s, there was a flurry of films with long titles. They often had at least three words. This included the likes of *Jis Desh Mein Ganga Behti Hai*, *Aap Aaye Bahar Ayee*, *Purab Aur Paschim* and *Mera Naam Joker.* These names were not just long but often hard to remember. Besides, it would be difficult when it came to pasting their posters. The lamp post was the place where these posters were most visible. If a film had a long name, it was impossible to read the name without difficulty. There was another peculiar problem to deal with. In India, film posters doubled up as food for cows as well. A slightly moody cow could chew up one half of a film's title, leaving the rest to the imagination of its onlookers.

Don would not have any of those issues. With three letters, it was an easy name to read. Besides, it was a title that sounded cool and yet comfortably desi. To Chandra, getting the title right was as important as any other component of the film. After the conversation with Manoj that morning, he was even more determined to call the film just *Don* without any suffix or prefix. Mr Don was certainly not a title that was music to his ears. This was his film and he was not going to change the title without reason.

CHAPTER FOUR

If there was one thing that was going to stand out about the way *Don* was made, it was the extent to which decisions were taken on an impulse. It's not as if there was not enough forethought or planning. In fact, Chandra was remarkably meticulous as a director and his hero was any director's best friend. It's just that the job on hand was complex and required thinking of a different nature. If there was a location, for instance, that looked exciting enough, a scene would promptly be shot there. How it would be woven into the film without looking contrived was a problem that could be addressed later.

Though Chandra was interested and curious about Amitabh's character in the lungi who chews paan incessantly, he surely did not imagine that it would captivate a nation for many years to come. One look at Salim–Javed's script and he knew this character was not anything similar to what Amitabh had ever played in his career so far. *Naya Din Nai Raat* was helpful in getting the talented actor to relate to what he was going to be like on screen, but the only familiar thing was that the character was called Vijay, a name that Amitabh was already identified with in *Zanjeer* and would soon be in *Deewar* and *Trishul.* Chandra knew that he had to get it right. This character was the crucial link in the film. He was smart, entertaining, slightly clumsy and naïve. It was a bit of an odd combination and it looked anything but easy.

He allowed his mind to drift and just observed everything that came his way. If he had to brief his star, it was imperative that he was crystal clear in his own mind. On the day Chandra sat down with Amitabh, he said exactly one sentence: 'Tiger, we need a Bhendi Bazaar look for the character with a colourful shirt and a lungi.' It was not an offensive remark and was stated with the objective of having a costume with a psychedelic look. Amitabh heard him out and did not say anything. Chandra decided that it was time to get his actor into that look. This was certainly not a bad time to do that.

In a moment, on Chandra's request, Amitabh called out for his driver. Nagesh, who by then was acquiring a reputation of being known as the star's driver, was a little confused when he was summoned with a tone of panic. The instructions to him were clear. He was to go to Amitabh's bungalow in Juhu and pick up a red shirt that Jaya would hand over. The lady had already been spoken to and tried not to be perplexed by this strange request in the middle of the day. As Nagesh zoomed out of Mehboob Studios' large premises, he was asked to return in a jiffy. Mehboob, to this day, has a large parking area where the drivers are constantly in animated conversation with one another. If there is some spare time, which is often the case, they either grab a nap under one of the many trees or indulge in a game of cards. It is a studio in the heart of the city and has a lot of nostalgic value. For *Don,* Mehboob was already the studio of preference.

With one part of the assignment being given to Nagesh,

Chandra now began looking for the dark green lungi. The studio was an impossible place to locate it and he decided to step out for a while. Traffic was somewhat heavy that day and when he crossed the road, he spotted a young man spreading his wares on the street. There was one lungi that caught the director's attention and after a bit of negotiation, he got it packed. The crucial costume for the street singer was now done. One part of it came from Amitabh's cupboard and the other off the streets in Bandra. In time, that character would come to be known as one of the most recognizable enactments of Amitabh. How the costume design for this crucial character was done on the spot was just one indication of the manner in which this film was going to be made. The director privately called this 'extempore working'. Indeed, it would be the highlight of this film. It was not as if Chandra was comfortable about working in this manner. It was just that the situation demanded it.

Chandra, for his part, said a quiet thank you to Prakash Mehra and that was not without reason. It was not the first time that a street singer would be used in Hindi cinema. Guru Dutt had employed it with great success in the 'Leke Pehla Pehla Pyaar' song from *CID* and more recently Prakash Mehra in *Zanjeer* with 'Deewane Hain Deewanon'. The latter was a huge success and the common link to both songs was the voice of Mohammed Rafi. Chandra was taken in by the song in Prakash's *Zanjeer* and was well aware of the chord it had struck with the audience. The music in *Zanjeer* was spoken of in the same breath as the quality of the film, and there was no reason why *Don* could not be as big as that.

'Yeh Mera Dil' was looking good and it pleased Amitabh and Helen. They were cautiously optimistic, though they knew the tune was catchy and it looked very slick. Amitabh,

Amitabh shooting for 'Yeh Hai Bambai Nagariya' outside the Gateway of India with Chandra watching

of course, had other films on the floor and was working on *Sholay* and *Deewar* apart from Yash Chopra's *Kabhi Kabhie*. This meant that he was travelling incessantly, with *Don* getting the smallest chunk of the star's time. Chandra was well aware of this and the moment there was some money available, he shot a couple of sequences for his project with his hero.

Amitabh had spent quite some time in Kashmir for *Kabhi Kabhie*. In fact, most of the film was shot there and the multi-starrer was being touted as the one to look out for. When his star was away, Chandra quietly showed his song and the scene after that to Salim and Javed. He thought he owed it to them and was also keen on their feedback. After all, it was their plot on the big screen.

When the duo watched what was barely five minutes of the film, they did not say too much. They gently complimented Chandra and said they were quite happy. The director was a relieved man and realized the role Manoj had played in the whole drama.

Less than two days later, Amitabh called Chandra from Kashmir in a tone that was gushing with excitement. 'Chandra, I have just got a telegram from Salim and Javed. They loved what they saw and say *Don* is of international calibre!' Chandra was touched and knew he was on the right path. If his stomach was churning, he did not show it. The sense of joy was almost uncontrollable.

CHAPTER FIVE

London was a huge tourist attraction in the 1970s for Indians. It had a lot of people who went there as migrants and did impressively. Hindi was easily heard in the lanes of the city and every family that had some money at its disposal thought it fit to go there for a holiday. More than anything else, shopping in the city was often the only reason to be there.

This was the phase when anything that was 'imported' was sought after. If you went to London, you would have to come back with fancy perfumes, chic sunglasses and contemporary (actually any Western!) apparels. Even today, stories abound in Bollywood on how stars of that time thought even combs from London were the best you could get in any part of the world. Who could have said that London would play such a big role in the success of *Don?*

When *Zanjeer* was released in 1973, Amitabh had a lot riding on the film. This was a script that was rejected without any hesitation by Rajkumar and Dev Anand. Like many films of the day, it failed to bring in the crowds over the first few days and its director, Prakash Mehra, who chose to produce the film, was a very worried man.

Once the good word about *Zanjeer* spread, there was no looking back and Amitabh had his first solo hit. While he was noticed in *Anand*, it was still a Rajesh Khanna film and he needed this break. By then, Amitabh was dating Jaya Bhaduri, who was a star in her own right. She had shared screen space with the likes of Sanjeev Kumar, Rajesh Khanna, who was the reigning star, Manoj Kumar and Jeetendra. Films like *Bansi Birju* and *Ek Nazar* had her with the still relatively unknown Amitabh.

Before *Zanjeer* was released, the two lovebirds decided that if the film was a hit, they would go abroad (actually London) on a holiday. If anyone was to tell Amitabh that two more films that year—*Abhimaan* and *Namak Haraam*—too would be successes, he would have well laughed it off. His focus was only on *Zanjeer* and the news that the audience loved the film. Chandra accompanied Amitabh and Jaya to Calcutta (now Kolkata) for the film's premiere. It was believed those days that if the police had to be called in to disperse the crowd at a theatre, it meant the film would be a huge hit. In this case, the crowd was beyond the control of the police. The image of the angry young man had struck the right chord with the masses. London just beckoned.

However, there was just one hitch. Harivansh Rai Bachchan, Amitabh's father, said the young couple would have to get married first. That did not seem like too much of a task and in less than a month of the release of *Zanjeer*, the two tied the knot at a friend's place at Skylark Apartments in Malabar Hill. There was some drama that morning when Amitabh barged into Chandra's bedroom at 7 a.m. and asked him to get ready. 'I am getting married,' was all he said. The next few hours were spent in just getting things organized for the wedding. It was a hush-hush affair with just close friends and relatives. Sanjay Gandhi flew in from Delhi, while the film fraternity had a few folks with Chandra being a prominent member. The wedding was exciting but there were other issues to handle like ensuring that the passports and visas for London came on time.

The good part about the trip to London was that the couple had a place to stay. Chandra's sister, Sudha, had been in the city for a while and her hospitality was well known. Chandra, by then, was extremely close to Amitabh and Jaya. After all, he played no small hand in the romance between the two with his

Chandra with sister Sudha and Amitabh on the sets of *Don*

apartment's balcony often being the meeting point. Chandra always found Amitabh's introverted nature a little odd and relentlessly pulled Jaya's leg about it. Nor did he spare a chance when it came to mimicking the tall man's baritone. The newly-weds were keen on Chandra holidaying with them and he agreed. Meanwhile, a big party was organized at 'Mangal', Amitabh's bungalow in Juhu. The guests were under the impression that the party was to celebrate the success of *Abhimaan*. That night, Amitabh, Jaya and Chandra boarded a flight to London. The party continued in the air when the Air India staff brought in a huge cake, organized by Mehmood's brother, Anwar Ali, and there was a lot of fun and frolic.

In London, the couple were no more than tourists and spent their time visiting places like the Buckingham Palace and Trafalgar Square. Chandra had been there several times and was more than willing to show them the nicer parts of the city. During the trip, they also made a stopover at Cambridge University. Harivansh Rai Bachchan had studied there and was keen that his son met the professor who had taught him. The professor's shelf had the literary work of Senior Bachchan. The word of *Zanjeer* being a success was yet to hit the international markets. People never really recognized Amitabh barring the odd question here and there. Little was he to anticipate that this would be among the last occasions when he would travel so freely without being mobbed.

Shopping was on the agenda and Amitabh, who even then was fond of good clothes, was taken to the best shops in Piccadilly Circus. One shop that Chandra had really liked was called Cecil Gee. They had some of the best menswear and he knew Amitabh would love it. On one sunny morning, the two decided to splurge.

When they entered the shop, the star was floored by the variety and the number of international brands. If he had it his way, he would have bought out the store. The shop attendants were an enthusiastic bunch and just loved Amitabh's voice. When it was time to try out the outfits, it was a bit of a surprise for the tall man when he was repeatedly touched around his waistline. He then realized that the attendant was gay and there was some laughter.

Amitabh liked a checked jacket as soon as he saw it and also picked up a dazzling, emerald green shirt. Clothes of this nature were not easily available in India and though they were expensive, they were also very cool and chic. Funnily enough, it was that same jacket and shirt that Amitabh wore in the 'Yeh Mera Dil' song. The star picked up the tab blissfully ignorant of the fact that the outfit would become synonymous with the song and the film a few years later.

When it came to accessories, Amitabh was fussy. He liked what he saw and both he and Chandra, another shopaholic, tried every pair of sunglasses they could lay their hands on. The one that really caught their fancy was the Ray-Ban night driving glasses. The brand was known to make safe night driving sunglasses and came with a pretty stiff price tag. Since it looked so appealing and would certainly attract attention, Amitabh decided to indulge. To his mind, this was a great accessory for his personal collection. In fact, it would be the pair that he would wear in the opening sequence of *Don*. The image of Amitabh, captured through the car's side mirror, zooms in on this pair and one can spot the Ray-Ban logo during that scene.

It was during this trip that the two men watched Francis Ford Coppola's *The Godfather*. The film had released in March that year and Marlon Brando's performance left them transfixed. If Mario Puzo's book was brilliant, the film was in no way inferior. To this day, Chandra believes that he was hugely inspired by that film when it came to the making of *Don*. Film lovers would agree with that statement without too much difficulty.

At that time, Nariman's precarious financial position or the possible bailout by making a film were still in a very distant future. That did not prevent Chandra from joyfully playing around with his camera and getting images of people walking around in London or just capturing the mood in the city. This included filming landmarks like the Big Ben, Westminster Abbey, Buckingham Palace and even the double decker buses. He was just having a good time with the camera. On one such random filming, a strange idea struck him out of the blue.

Yes, there was no question of discussing work on a trip like this. However, Chandra had a word with Amitabh on what was playing at the back of his mind. 'Tiger, why can't I get a couple of shots of you in London? We could have you just walking around a few locations and get a feel of you in a new country,' he said to the attentive star. Amitabh was immediately taken in by the idea. Deep inside, he was kicked since it gave him a chance to move around in fancy clothes in a city that he was already beginning to love.

The following day Chandra accompanied by Amitabh and his camera, went to the iconic British Museum. Over the next few minutes, they had shots of the star coming out of the impressive structure and walking through the city's streets. There were shots of him crossing traffic signals and entering busy streets. There was something that was still missing and Chandra was not able to put a finger on it. He then figured that the object of anyone's attention back home in India was a sports car. There was no better time to get an image of Amitabh emerging from a building and getting into an expensive sports car. Luckily, Chandra's friend in London was willing to lend his car for a while and some pretty slick shots were filmed. No one had a clue about what to do with the filmed material. Certainly not Chandra, who packed his camera very carefully after the job was done. He would reach out for that camera less than two years later to retrieve some of that footage.

CHAPTER SIX

The drive from Dar es Salaam in Tanzania to Nairobi in Kenya is a huge tourist attraction since it offers spectacular views of both Mount Meru and Mount Kilimanjaro. Even if there are enough flights connecting the two cities, those with an appetite for nature often settle for this beautiful drive.

In late 1962, *Dr No* was released in Nairobi. The film, based on Ian Fleming's novel that hit the stands four years before the release, was really drawing the crowds. Chandra Barot, still a couple of months shy of twenty one, was intrigued by the talk of this debut James Bond film. The young man had a steady day job at Barclays Bank in Dar es Salaam and was finding it difficult to squeeze out time to watch the film. Besides, watching the film meant going to Nairobi. At a distance of over 900 km, it entailed a twelve-hour drive by road.

One Friday evening, as Chandra was having dinner with his group of friends, an impromptu plan to watch *Dr No* in Nairobi was made. They had four motorcycles and there were eight of them. The following morning, at the crack of dawn, they left Dar es Salaam. The adventurous bunch had no idea how they were going to get back to work on Monday morning. For now, the attraction of watching Sean Connery on screen was the priority.

They reached Nairobi around 7 p.m. after a break for lunch. Importantly, this was just in time for the evening show which had a running time of just less than 110 minutes. The eight youngsters were transfixed by what they saw. The joy of watching Bond on screen lighting a cigarette was the most stylish visual of the movie. When the audience heard, 'Bond, James Bond', there was a stunned silence. This clearly was trendy filmmaking at its best.

Ursula Andress as Honey Rider set the hearts of the young men in Nairobi on fire. That unforgettable visual of her emerging from the water in a white bikini was as important to them as it was to millions of viewers who are still gushing about it five decades later. Once the film was over, they spent the night at a friend's place in the Kenyan capital. Less than twenty-four hours after leaving Dar es Salaam, they were finding their way back with memories of what was to be a life changing experience for at least one of the eight.

Chandra was born in February 1942 and had finished his Senior Cambridge examination in 1959. Having spent all his life in Dar es Salaam, he had little connection with India barring speaking Gujarati at home. In fact, his spoken Hindi was nothing to write home about. He had heard a little bit about the JJ School of Art in Mumbai and thought it was a good idea to study there. Gifted with the ability to draw well, joining art school was a logical progression.

Dar es Salaam was a city that had a lot of Gujaratis then. This was the migratory population that had left India to seek their fortune elsewhere. The city was extremely cosmopolitan and a young man growing up there was easily Westernised by nature.

Between his Senior Cambridge examinations and the results, Chandra had about six to seven months from June to December. There was very little to do and his father mentioned an interesting job at Barclays. There was no pressure on him but he decided to apply. As luck would have it, he was picked up and he started work almost immediately.

What was to be a time-filler of a job turned out to be his profession for nine years. Barclays had a training centre with about three hundred students and Chandra found it was just a joy to hang out with people of a similar mindset. They worked hard and spent a lot of time together after work as well. It also suited Chandra's personality since he was a man who liked to dress well and flaunt the fancy accessories that he possessed in no small number. After all, he was making more than a little bit of money. As a cashier, his salary was 2,800 shillings or 140 pounds. In his 9 a.m. to 5 p.m. schedule, he would spend a lot of his spare time sketching and painting. Some of his work included caricatures of people he met casually and those he worked with.

Life was on track till the mid-1960s when Tanzania, like many other parts of Africa, was becoming dangerous to live in. Racial riots were becoming common and suddenly this place was not the one that its inhabitants were familiar with. Soon, they began to immigrate to other countries and, in many instances, thought it was a good idea to rediscover their lost roots like those in faraway India.

Chandra's manager at the bank too was moving and thought his junior should do likewise. The Englishman gave him a strong recommendation letter and advised him to get his act together quickly. For Chandra, this was not an easy decision but given the lack of options, he knew it was best to move elsewhere.

His brother Pratap, who was employed with British Airways in London, asked Chandra to come over. Taking the recommendation letter and finding a job in London seemed like a good idea. Also on the agenda was to take a two week vacation in India, where his sister Kamal was already a well-known singer. Kamal was only too happy to have her brother over. That trip in 1967 was to be critical in the time to come.

In 1964, Chandra had come to Mumbai for a holiday. He quite liked the city and its pace. During that trip, he spent a lot of time with his brother, Pratap, who was then married to Sitara Devi, the eminent kathak dancer. The lady was Dilip Kumar's rakhi sister and shared a wonderful relationship with some of the Hindi film industry's best names. Chandra was introduced to Kalyanji–Anandji, who had migrated from Kutch and a young man called Prem Chopra, who was just starting to get noticed as the villain to look out for.

Chandra was taken to the musical session of *Woh Kaun Thi* during that trip and was briefly introduced to Manoj Kumar, the film's lead male artist. For most Indians growing up in East Africa in the 1960s, the only connection to India was often Bollywood. There was a sense of awe and amazement about stars and people were mesmerized by what they saw on screen. Being in Mumbai meant there was a chance to meet some of these stars. Saira Banu, after the success of *Junglee*, was a rage in that part of Africa, apart from Dilip Kumar, Raj Kapoor and the handsome Dev Anand. In fact, when Chandra was leaving for Mumbai, one of his friends requested a picture of Saira Banu. He said yes not knowing how he was going to get it.

When he conveyed this to Sitara, she just smiled without promising anything. A couple of days later, she took the young man to Dilip's house where he was introduced to a gentleman by the name of Bimal Roy. Chandra's lack of interest in films resulted in a cursory hello to one of Bollywood's finest film directors who, by then, had already made *Do Bigha Zamin, Devdas, Madhumati, Sujata, Parakh* and, more recently, *Bandini.*

Chandra decided to carry a gift for Dilip, an elephant's tusk from Africa. That aroused some serious curiosity from onlookers. When they asked the man if he was from Africa, he replied in the affirmative in his broken Hindi. Dilip came a few minutes later and warmly greeted Sitara. He was shooting for *Leader* and was spending a lot of time in the studios. In the midst of that meeting, he invited Sitara and her brother-in-law to come to Mehboob Studios the following day for a party. The incentive was a huge surprise awaiting them.

The surprise was Kirk Douglas and it was a party to remember. The industry's biggies were all there and Chandra saw the likes of Shammi Kapoor, Raj Kapoor, Dilip Kumar and Manoj Kumar. He was curious and not one bit awestruck. He just wanted to take care of the photo request. Then he saw Saira entering. Chandra rushed to her and, after a brief introduction, said he had to have her picture clicked. The lady gracefully accepted and the young man heaved a sigh of relief. In just over a decade, the friendship between Dilip, Saira and Chandra would take shape. To this day, that has remained.

When Chandra came back to India in 1967, he again met

Chandra in the mid-1970s

Kalyanji–Anandji. The duo invited him to watch the trial of *Upkar*. The film was scheduled for release in a few days and there was already some hype around the project. Manoj's 'Mr Bharat' image would gain form and shape from this film. With patriotism being a key feature, there was a feeling this would strike the right chord with the audience.

Chandra was blissfully ignorant of the fact that Manoj was sitting behind him at the trial. Besides, Manoj had met the man from Africa very casually three years ago and had almost no recollection of that. In the midst of the film, Chandra was getting a little restless and did not really relate to one particular scene. 'This is absolutely ridiculous. How can someone show something like this?' he commented. Manoj certainly heard that and was quite taken in by the young man's observation when he spoke to him after the trial. 'You seem like a smart guy. Why don't you stay back here and work with me?' he asked Chandra. The offer was a salary of ₹500 per month, which meant he would take home ₹485 after a small tax deduction. The young man politely declined as he had already decided on London. Manoj left his number just in case he was interested.

A few days later, Chandra took the flight to London. The scout for a job began almost immediately. Things, however, were anything but easy. Racial discrimination was at its peak and there was no luck for him. Six months passed and Chandra was frustrated and starting to get worried. Something had to be done quickly.

One evening, after returning to his brother's apartment, he knew he he had to reach a decision. It was another fruitless day with a job seeming very elusive. He reached out for the phone and called Manoj at home. The director was polite and asked about Chandra's well-being. 'Is your job offer still open?' he asked Manoj. The answer was what Chandra was hoping to hear. In a few days, he was on a flight to Mumbai with a job in an industry he knew nothing about.

When Chandra landed, *Upkar* was at the fag end of production. The film was the biggest hit of 1967 and at the Filmfare Awards the following year, it won seven awards. Manoj himself won four, which included ones for the Best Film and the Best Director.

In 1968, Manoj started work on *Purab Aur Paschim* which would be released two years later. The man was on a roll and there was no stopping him. Chandra joined him as an assistant director and worked with Manoj between 1967 and 1974 till *Don* came into his life. During that period, he worked on *Purab Aur Paschim*, *Yaadgaar* and by the time *Shor* was released in 1972, he was chief assistant director. It was on the sets of *Shor* in 1971 that Chandra met the young, talented Jaya Bhaduri. After *Shor*, which was another huge success, came *Roti Kapada Aur Makaan* in 1974, which was the biggest hit of the year.

Chandra was a part of the 'School of Manoj Kumar' which included eight assistant directors. These eight individuals rode the success wave with Manoj in what was an unbelievable run at the box-office. Not even in his wildest dreams did Chandra anticipate that he would turn director so quickly. For the banker from Africa, the run in Mumbai's film industry was just starting.

CHAPTER SEVEN

There was no doubt that the first scene of *Don* would need to be absolutely gripping. Chandra was aware of that, but was still unclear about how and where to shoot it. The Bond touch was necessary and he began examining various options. He did not get very far and decided to take some time off. Getting out of the city for a while seemed like a good idea.

Deciding where to go was the easiest thing. He picked up the phone and reached out to Manmohan Shetty, who had a bungalow in Lonavla. Shetty, who was already making his name in the film processing business, was Chandra's good friend. His bungalow was a major getaway for stars who wanted some privacy. Chandra just had to check if the place was available that weekend. It was and he quickly made plans to leave the following day.

The drive from Chandra's apartment in plush Peddar Road to Lonavla was expected to take about an hour and a half depending on the traffic. It was a beautiful day and the time of the year that most people in the city longed for. It was after Mumbai's muggy second summer and just before the onset of winter.

Traffic that day was a little heavy because of the weekend crowd stepping out. Once Chandra got past Sion and Chembur, he decided to get into top gear. It was a good time for some music and he played some vintage English pop from the 1960s. As he entered what is today Navi Mumbai, something caught the corner of his eye. Just before CIDCO, the sprawling land to his left had a vast expanse of grass that had been uncut for a while. It was the colour that gave him a kick although it was not unusual for the grass to have that burnt shade during that time of the year. In one moment, he knew the location for the opening sequence was under his belt.

This was the sequence that would lead to the titles and, over the next few days, Chandra began discussing in detail the whole thing with Nariman. The cameraman loved the location and told Chandra to get cracking since the season might not hold out.

Getting Amitabh ready for this shot was the main thing. Deep down, Chandra was clear that he would use a foreign car. It just seemed to make sense given the star's role in the film. The moment Chandra saw the red car that was to be used, he was over the moon. This was as beautiful as anything he had driven.

Amitabh had to be dressed impeccably and that meant a suit and a bow tie which would go well with the Ray-Ban glasses. Even the three villains who confront Amitabh had to be well turned out and two of them were in smart, formal jackets. The other was casually dressed to convey a mean look.

By then, Kalyanji–Anandji had composed the music for

the scene. It had a great rhythm and was appropriate for the sequence. Chandra thought it was fine if that track could lead to some background music for the titles as well. His musician duo did not fail to impress and the music for that opening shot and the titles that follow are etched in the mind of the viewer to date.

The shot entailed the hero's car driving at top speed through the grass before he steps out with a briefcase that has the gold. Chandra was finding it hard to take his eyes off the car and was keen on getting behind the wheel for the shot. Amitabh gave in quite easily. Actually, a close look at the shot and some relentless effort with the pause button on the DVD player at home shows Chandra for a little more than a fraction of a second. It was not the only shot in the film where the director would appear.

The objective was to stun the audience since they had not seen Amitabh in a role where he would blow up the villains without a thought. The idea of the bomb in the suitcase had that cool, Western feel where Don never leaves anything to chance. Besides, the gun would never be wielded by the hero. Chandra wanted a great one-liner and Salim–Javed gave him more than what he had asked for. *Raj Singh, kya tumhe maut se dar nahin lagta?* (Raj Singh, aren't you afraid of death?) is the hero's question when the three men try to double-cross him.

To Amitabh's fans, this was the hero they had never seen before. The angry young man image is what they had gotten used to and this ruthless killer image was a bolt from the blue. Chandra was convinced it was the perfect way to start and set the tempo and he was not wrong. Later, when he saw the shot with Nariman, they looked at each other quietly. Nothing was said. The shot was cleared instantly.

The extent to which Chandra's friends helped him with *Don* made the process of shooting that much easier. He adopted a simple plan. Whenever another film was being shot, he would request the producer to retain the set for a day or two before pulling it down. This would entail a payment of a marginal fee for those two days. That was pretty much what Chandra and Nariman could afford.

One film that Chandra was keeping tabs on was *Majboor*. Ravi Tandon was directing this film and it was scheduled for a late 1974 release. When *Don* was conceived, there was no clarity on how long it would take before the film would be released. *Majboor*, a remake of a 1970 English film, *Zigzag*, had no such problem and shooting was on track. The only way for Chandra to get the best out of *Majboor* was to work his scenes around that film and ensure that the shooting of *Don* was as flexible as possible.

One reason for *Majboor* not facing any pressure on finances was the presence of its producer, Premji. The man had already produced huge hits like Raj Khosla's *Mera Saaya*, Rajesh Khanna's 1971 blockbuster *Dushman* and Dharmendra's *Dost*. The last one had released in April that year. Over the next few years, he would produce *Immaan Dharam* that starred Amitabh and Shashi Kapoor. When Chandra asked Premji for permission to use his sets for a couple of sequences, he did not realize that help from the producer would come in other ways as well.

One of the more important sequences in *Don* was to be shot in a hospital when Vijay, the street singer, needs to make his way into the gang. Zeenat was a key component of this scene and she aids the process ofVijay escaping from the hospital in a beard, which is meant to be a disguise. This hospital set was

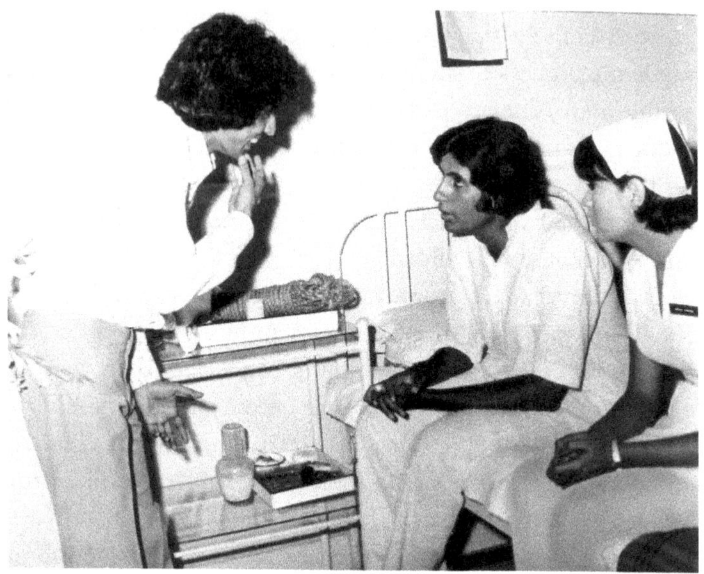

Chandra directing Amitabh and Zeenat in the hospital scene

what the crew of *Majboor* had put up at Mehboob Studios. The sequence of *Don* was shot quickly before Chandra could decide what the next scene would be.

Likewise, the confrontation between Pran and Iftekhar after the former gets out of jail was on the sets of *Majboor*. This was just the moment before Iftekhar sets out to try and apprehend the gang. It was a juggling act for Chandra to shoot his scenes in an order that only he would understand. Again, the scene with a bare-chested Amitabh in a sauna with his gun was from what was left on the sets of *Majboor*. In each of these instances, the set was slightly modified to ensure that the audience would not notice anything similar. Interestingly, the scene in the sauna has the camera zooming into a gun which is actually a cigarette lighter. It was one of

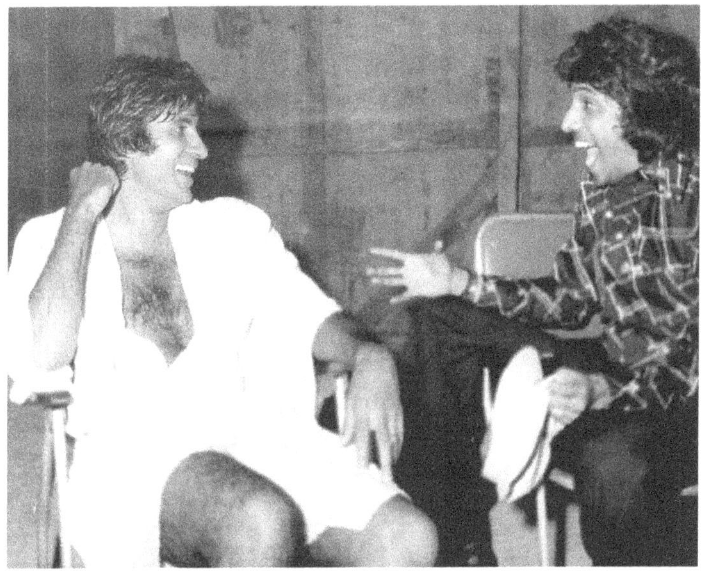

Chandra and Amitabh on the sets of *Don*—this is the scene where the actor is in the sauna bath

the things that Chandra had picked from one of the multitude of London's curios shops during one of his trips. He liked the way it looked and fitted into the gadget theme of Bond.

Even the sequence where Amitabh first notices the red diary in the film was courtesy Premji. This is the moment when it is conveyed to the hero that the diary has details of the gang's network across the world. The other man on the screen was Kamal Kapoor, who had a small role in *Deewar* and was Narang in *Don*. He had played a police officer in films like *Sachaa Jhutha, Mehboob Ki Mehndi* and *Khotte Sikkay*. In time, he would be seen in other Amitabh starrers like *Namak Halaal, Nastik, Mard* and *Toofan*. Kamal, who passed way in 2010, was Goldie Behl's grandfather.

When Chandra was shooting a key sequence between Iftekhar and the street singer, he suddenly realized that he needed a picture of Amitabh. This was the night sequence where Iftekhar calls on Vijay at home to brief him on the plan to be the police informer. Here, Iftekhar, the cop, shows him a picture of the real Don. The street singer is stunned when he notices the uncanny resemblance. This picture of Amitabh was taken from Premji and was shot on the sets of *Majboor*.

Premji had made his fortune and owned property outside Mumbai as well. This included an old-fashioned bungalow located in Mira Road, a suburb that is just over an hour by the local train from Churchgate. It had large doors and high ceilings. This seemed like the right place for Pran to move in after his jail experience. Incidentally, this was the sequence where Amitabh, who is on the run, meets Pran for the first time. As the hero slithers in, he barely escapes Pran's attention. As the cops come and go, Pran and Amitabh speak to each other briefly before the former shows him the way out. If Chandra was relieved about how he had saved money by shooting on used sets, he would now need to think a little harder for a whole host of outdoor sequences. Options were limited and he did not want to compromise on the slickness of the film. His mind worked as fast as it had in the recent past.

CHAPTER EIGHT

The making of *Don* through the mid-1970s coincided with the construction of one of the city's most iconic structures. When Sea Rock Hotel opened its doors to visitors in 1978, it marked the emergence of a landmark that the city would relate to for a decade and a half. Bandra, already referred to as the queen of the suburbs, now had its own fancy hotel to boast of and there was no need to look towards south Mumbai for the Taj or the Oberoi.

Chandra quite liked the way the hotel looked and it seemed ideal to shoot a couple of scenes as it was being constructed. It had large pillars and tonnes of construction material that just lay around. That was not all. It had innumerable entry and exit points that were perfect for a good fight sequence. He figured it would look even better if he could shoot at night.

Chandra decided that the scene where the situation of the mistaken identity was corrected had to be shot at the construction site. Zeenat, blissfully ignorant of the street singer replacing the villain, is determined on avenging her brother Ramesh's gory death. When she sees Vijay's memory coming back, she is clear that the time to kill him could not be more opportune.

The scene starts off with Amitabh making his way into Iftekhar's house as he adopts the rather dangerous *upar se neeche* (from top to bottom) method. Till then, the gang

Amitabh deep in thought on the sets of *Don*

members are still worried over their star member's recovery from his memory lapse. He is suddenly back to being the cool, gun-toting person they were so used to seeing.

Amitabh climbing into Iftekhar's house was shot late in the night in one of Bandstand's tall structures. It had over a dozen floors and suited Chandra's image of a classic high-rise building. As the hero unexpectedly spots Zeenat, all hell breaks loose. Her one-point agenda is to kill him and she draws out a sharp knife to cut the rope. The hero aimlessly falls into thin air before landing in a swimming pool. It is here where the chase begins between the two of them. That shot was filmed in Sea Rock's parking lot. A closer look will reveal that the lady in the frame is not always Zeenat. When there is a bit of action involved, her place is taken over by a duplicate and he (it was not a she!) is Hussain, a professional stuntman. Luckily, the shot in the film has Zeenat sporting a boy-cut and there was really nothing much to do on the hairdo. Hussain is seen many a time later in the film doubling up for Zeenat.

Shooting in a hotel was a good idea since it gave the film a slicker look and the stars some privacy. Besides, a scene that required the presence of a lot of people was tailor-made for a shot in a hotel. Sea Rock again was the preferred choice for the filming of the 'Main Hoon Don' song. The difference was that, unlike the fight sequence between Amitabh and Zeenat, this was to be shot indoors. It had a dancing Amitabh whose identity is unknown to everyone in that room. He dances energetically to a fast song that has a lot of people dressed in interesting and varied outfits. Soon, he hits the dance floor with some women. A prominent absentee here is Zeenat and Dev Anand had no small role to play in that.

When Chandra saw the banquet hall in Sea Rock, he liked the vast space available and the cool, business look. Perfect for a gangster-moll kind of a scene, he thought. He was quite right and the thought that a key scene had already been filmed when the hotel was still under construction was not far from his mind. 'This film has been in the making for a while,' he said to himself in a slightly worried tone. In fact, another important scene was shot in the hotel with Don on a staircase. Here, he meets Zeenat for the first time and is impressed with her fighting abilities. He utters the immortal *Mujhe junglee billiyan pasand hain* (I like wild cats). What goes unnoticed is that Amitabh and Zeenat are never shown together in that scene. If the hero was in a plush hotel mouthing his dialogue, his leading lady's shot was at Mehboob Studios. She just says 'Thank you, Don' and the two scenes were merged at the time of post-production.

Through the 1970s and a good part of the 1980s, Sea Rock was the five-star hotel for Bollywood. It had a health club that was second to none with local Bandra resident, Rekha, being a regular visitor. Rama Bans, already a name in the fitness circuit, was synonymous with the hotel and counted several stars among her clientele. With a stunning promenade that faced the sea, the hotel was a star attraction for many years. It had stars meeting the press for interviews in the coffee shop. Old timers still swear by the hotel's revolving restaurant and unforgettable filmi parties.

The Mumbai bomb blasts saw Sea Rock becoming one of the casualties with a significant part of the hotel destroyed. Labour issues did not help its cause and it was razed to the ground after the Taj group acquired it. In a few years, it would bear a new look, though to the city's taxi and auto rickshaw drivers, Sea Rock Hotel still holds a serious and meaningful emotional connect.

Like Sea Rock, Chandra shot quite extensively at Hotel Horizon, a property that faced the city's Juhu beach. It was a smaller hotel and a perfect hangout. It had large suites that faced the sea and though the hotel lost quite a bit of its charm later, there remain people from a bygone era who still wish they could stop by for a cup of coffee when they want to relive a bit of the past. Sadly, the hotel has been demolished and nothing from the past remains.

It was a large suite that was chosen for the only interaction between Zeenat and her brother Ramesh. It is the scene where she walks in with the flight tickets and begs her brother to get out of what he is doing. The image of Ramesh, played by Sharad Kumar (also known as Jolly Sharad Kumar), holding a mug of beer and gently inhaling a cigarette as he watches the sun on the beach remains an abiding image. Dressed in a night suit, Sharad was asked by Chandra to wear that worried and harassed look on his face.

Sharad was actually working for Air India when *Don* came his way. He was recommended for the film by Chandra's brother, Pratap, who thought the young man would do well in a fleeting appearance. The long sideburns were the result of being a huge Elvis Presley fan. After the film, Sharad moved to Canada to seek his fortune. He is still remembered for that cameo in *Don* and being the reason for the 'Yeh Mera Dil' song. Film lovers would recall him playing a brief role in *Sholay* and *Joroo Ka Ghulam*, a 1972 release. Sharad also lent his voice to the 'Do Lafzon Ki Hai Dil Ki Kahani' song from *The Great Gambler*.

Visitors specifically liked the Horizon's swimming pool. It was large, clean and one could spend hours there. For

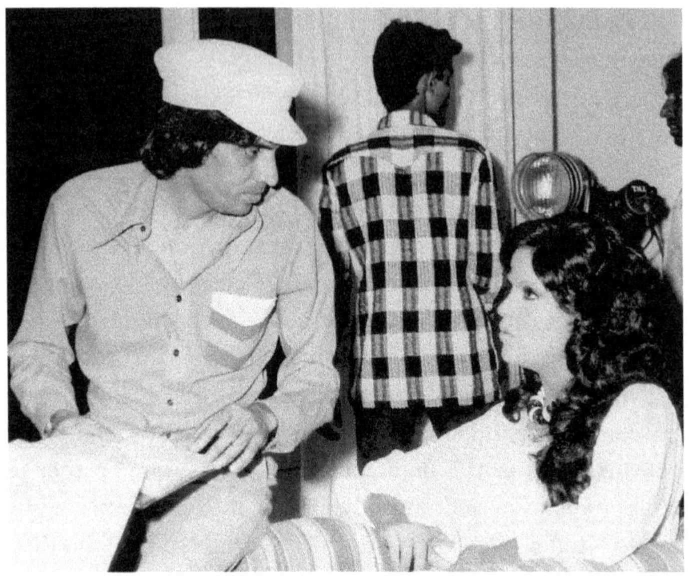

Chandra with Zeenat at Hotel Horizon on the sets of *Don*

the second half of the film, the script allowed for Amitabh to frolic in the pool with his lady. Chandra was taken in by Horizon and knew it would be a quick sequence to wrap up. It had the hero in the pool with Zeenat and a bit of drama then follows from Don's jilted lover who tells Macmohan (just Mac in the film) that she is convinced that there is something fishy.

Once that shot was in the bag, Chandra and the rest of the crew were pleasantly surprised by the unexpected visit of a smart, young pilot. Rajiv Gandhi, then with Indian Airlines, was flying on the Delhi–Mumbai route and decided to call on Amitabh. Horizon was not terribly far from the city's domestic airport in Santacruz and Rajiv had a couple of hours to kill. Keeping Rajiv company was his charming wife,

Sonia, and their two adorable children, Rahul and Priyanka. Lunch was served on the sets as the two kids were clearly enjoying Amit Uncle's company. Chandra had a good feeling about the film and chuckled to himself when he suddenly thought of what Nariman had said to him about the need to develop his own style of direction. He quietly watched the sea and could not take his eyes off the waves that were pounding the sand. There was still a lot of work to be done.

CHAPTER NINE

A little box was delivered on the sets of Rakesh Kumar's *Do Aur Do Paanch* in Filmistan Studio in early 1978. It was in the name of Amitabh Bachchan. The actor was busy with the shooting of the film and did not bother to check the contents of the box immediately. Once his sequence was shot, he had a look and was visibly excited.

Over the next half hour, the crew of *Do Aur Do Paanch* was riveted to the screen as they watched 'Yeh Hai Bambai Nagaria'. It was shown eight times and they could not have enough of it. Rakesh, who had already directed Amitabh in films like *Khoon Pasina* and *Mr Natwarlal* and later *Yaarana*, was thrilled by what he saw. He warmly congratulated Amitabh and so did Shashi, Hema and Parveen.

Funnily enough, the box took a while before it came back to Chandra. Given that he was so involved in *Don*, a call from Rekha gushing about the song was a pleasant surprise. 'It looks so different. You have done a great job,' she said. Chandra thanked her profusely and could not help but chuckle for a moment. After all, Amitabh had been a little reluctant to shoot that song and not without reason.

By the time 'Yeh Hai Bambai Nagaria' was being shot, Amitabh's image was not just of a bankable artist but of one who had an image far removed from the character in the song. This required him to pose in a lungi and a bright shirt coupled with oily hair and relentlessly chewing paan. He was not sure what this would do to his image or, for that matter, what the reaction of his audience would be. *'Chandra, tu kya mujeh lungi pahnake Taj ke baahar raaste pe nachvayega?'* asked Amitabh? (Will you make me dance on the street outside the Taj in a lungi?) Chandra convinced him and told him it was merely in line with the character in *Don* and there was no reason to panic. Amitabh took his director's word for it and in time, it was proven that it was indeed the best thing that he could have done.

The song called for a sense of ingenuity. Well-known locations like Bandra and Churchgate formed the lyrics of the song and Chandra knew it would be next to impossible to shoot in these areas. His star was now a known face and the crowds would be tough to manage. He chose to start filming the song outside the iconic Taj Mahal Hotel and moved to the nearby Oberoi where the Marine Drive formed the perfect background. When that part of the song was done, he had to quickly decide where to wrap up the next part.

Juhu beach was a good location, thought Chandra. The next day, under bright sunlight, the crew descended on the beach and began filming what remained of the song. Over the last few days, Chandra wondered how to get past filming in Bandra and Churchgate and there seemed to be no solution. A casual visit to the beach gave him the answer. He watched the rows of shops selling all kinds of food and trinkets. What caught his attention was a young man trying to sell something that looked colourful to a bunch of tourists. It was a set of

Amitabh and the two kids dancing to 'Yeh Hai Bambai Nagaria' outside Taj Mahal Hotel

Amitabh at Juhu beach dancing to 'Yeh Hai Bambai Nagaria'

picture postcards that had the names of various landmarks in the city like the Gateway in addition to the elusive Bandra and Churchgate. He remembered to tell the young man to be around when the song was being shot. Today, as one watches the song, it is hard to miss Amitabh pointing towards those picture postcards as he mouths Bandra and Churchgate.

Though Chandra had been in the industry for a while, there were still some people who did not know him too well. The music in *Don* changed that. When Nargis Dutt called Chandra late one evening, she was hugely excited after having watched 'Yeh Hai Bambai Nagaria'. She then insisted that her niece, Zahida Hussain, take a look at it too. Zahida had already shared screen space with Dev Anand in *Gambler* and *Prem Pujari*.

A couple of days later, Chandra accompanied Dilip Kumar to Nashik where Saira was shooting for *Kala Aadmi*, a film directed by Ramesh Lakhanpal. By then, Chandra was very close to Dilip and his family and was a regular at their Bandra bungalow. Sunil Dutt, the hero of the film, was also there with Nargis and Zahida and pleasantries were exchanged. In the middle of some serious conversation, Sunil casually told Dilip that both his wife, Nargis, and her niece, Zahida, were crazy about a song in an upcoming film called *Don*. 'These girls have gone crazy about the number. *Yeh Barot ladka ne to kamaal kar diya* (This Barot boy has worked wonders),' he said, quite unaware of Chandra's presence there. Saira could not stop laughing as she told Sunil that the gentleman mentioned was seated in their midst. A sheepish Sunil was embarrassed as he asked Chandra if he could see the song. The director sportingly agreed.

It was a tremendous source of relief to Chandra that another song, in addition to 'Yeh Mera Dil', had taken off. Rejoicing in the feedback that was coming his way, he least anticipated that Nariman would come with a mini time bomb. 'Bachu, we have a bit of a problem. Zeenat will not be around for a month,' he said as Chandra listened aghast. The lady was scheduled to shoot with Dev for *Kalabaaz*. Directed by Ashok Roy, the film required Zeenat to be away in Shimla for a month. The issue was that Chandra was all set to shoot the 'Main Hoon Don' number and there was no way it could be done without Zeenat. Besides, the romantic relationship between Amitabh and Zeenat was established in the film and the song was the critical component to what lay ahead in the theme. There was no point in trying to convince

Zeenat since she had already committed her dates to the *Kalabaaz* team.

Chandra reached out to Salim and Javed who were remarkably calm. In a matter of minutes, the duo came up with a practical solution. The scene before the song has Amitabh chatting with Iftekhar and revealing the fact that a huge get-together of the gang leaders had been planned for the following day. Iftekhar promises to be there with his police battalion and, in that sense, the film is scheduled to end with that scene. Of course, Iftekhar's death in the crucial sequence changes everything and the film then progresses into an equally gripping second half.

In the telephonic chat between Amitabh and Iftekhar, the

Nariman, Amitabh and Chandra during the making of *Don*

latter gently requests the hero to ensure that Zeenat is not around. His logic is simple. It is a police raid and he does not want to take any chances. Amitabh agrees and Zeenat is nowhere to be seen in the song. Actually, not quite. In the second verse of the song, Amitabh removes Zeenat's picture from his coat pocket and takes a good look at it before romantically singing '*Arre yaaron ka wo yaar hoon, Yaari mein ye jaan luta de jo*'. In one stroke, her absence was addressed through a quick and timely solution. The other point that stands out about the song was Amitabh's outfit that, in time, would become one of the best known images of *Don*.

If the objective was to make a racy film, the theme for *Don* was perfect. It was always meant to be a Bond kind of a film. The only difference was that no Bond film ever had songs. From the first day of shooting, Chandra was clear that this had to be a thriller with the songs being what he still calls 'the hand brakes'. That was not such a great thought and the director worked doubly hard to make sure every song was integral to the film's plot. If he had it his way, *Don* would probably have had no music. Chandra knew only too well how directors in the past had exploited a good and strong musical score to their advantage and he was not about to rewrite the rule book. There was too much at stake.

Having worked with Manoj for several years, Chandra had closely observed how his mentor behaved during the recording sessions of his films. The results were wonderful. Be it 'Mere Desh Ki Dharti' or 'Kasme Waade Pyar Wafa' from *Upkar* or 'Main Na Bhoolunga' and 'Haye Haye Yeh Majboori' from *Roti Kapda Aur Makaan*, good music in a film was often more than half the battle won. Manoj would spend hours at the song recordings. In the past, those like Raj Kapoor, Guru Dutt and Raj Khosla had been no different. Every film of theirs had great songs and Chandra knew that a strong music score could make a huge difference.

Coming from a musical background too helped. Chandra's father played the dilruba, a stringed instrument and considered among the toughest to play. Even if Chandra could not sing, he had a wonderful ear for music and that helped.

Don had four songs and the tight script seemed appropriate for that. When Chandra had to shoot 'Jiska Mujhe Tha Intezaar', he wanted his heroine to wear an outfit that stood out. Incidentally, it is this number that remains Chandra's favourite in the film. Choosing Zeenat's costume for this song

P.L. Raj, Chandra, Nutan Barot, Amitabh and Macmohan discussing 'Jiska Mujhe Tha Intezaar'. Nutan was the assistant director in *Don*

was a tricky one. This song was to lead into the scene where she is all set to kill Amitabh for having killed her brother. The plan is to lure him and then knock him off.

As Chandra repeatedly kept saying the word revenge to himself, he thought it was common sense to have a cactus plant there. It would symbolize the whole story about wanting to seek revenge and kill this wicked man. As Chandra's mind began looking for ideas, he drifted to thinking of his trip to London in 1974 where he had hung out with a bunch of friends.

In the middle of one aimless window shopping, he had stopped at a bookstore to see what had hit the market recently. The big one was *The Pirate* written by Harold Robbins. It was doing well and, in 1978, would be made into a four hour film to be aired on television. The book's cover had

A still from the 'Jiska Mujhe Tha Intezaar' song

its main character, a lady, in a sizzling emerald-blue outfit. Chandra loved that shade and that was the inspiration for Zeenat's outfit.

The filming of 'Jiska Mujhe Tha Intezaar' was not without its shares of hitches. Zeenat had been missing from 'Main Hoon Don' and Chandra faced a similar situation for this song too when Arpana Choudhary, who played Anita, had to leave to shoot a Punjabi film. Prior to *Don*, Arpana was

Chandra with Asha Bhosle during the recording of 'Yeh Mera Dil'

seen in films like *Aaj ki Taaza Khabar*, *Ajnabee*, *Warrant* and *Ponga Pandit*.

This was not the time to ask the writers what could be done. Chandra used the camera to his advantage and got close-ups of Arpana before she left. These were then interspersed with the actual song. Viewers may note that while Arpana is with the rest of the gang in the song, she is never spotted with Amitabh and Zeenat. The camera continuously zooms in on her drink and a livid Arpana as she watches Amitabh and Zeenat dance. She had been jilted and the expression on her face conveys frustration and helplessness.

For the music of *Don*, Amitabh's voice was lent by Kishore Kumar. If it was Asha for 'Yeh Mera Dil', and it was Lata Mangeshkar and Kishore for 'Jiska Mujhe Tha Intezaar'. With the songs for *Don* having been filmed, Chandra's next task was to reach out to HMV, the most well-known record company then. It was a big brand name and he knew he would have to work really hard to convince them to buy the music to this film. For one thing, Chandra was up against the best of directors. He knew *Don* had Amitabh and Kalyanji–Anandji. However, this was HMV and they had worked with the biggest names of Bollywood like Raj Kapoor, Nasir Hussain and R.D. Burman and possessed a fine catalogue. Chandra had to pitch very, very hard and he knew it would be challenging.

He listened to his four songs time and again and knew that clinching a record deal with HMV was critical. These songs would then be aired on Radio Ceylon and the Ameen Sayani-hosted *Binaca Geetmala*. With the quality of music in *Don* and the feedback he got from various quarters, he was optimistic and yet nervous. If someone had told him then that another song would need to be recorded and it would be that number that would change everyone's career forever, he would have certainly laughed it off. It required Manoj Kumar's foresight and maturity to lend that once-over for the film's music. He did that in a dramatic fashion.

CHAPTER TEN

It takes about forty-five minutes, or approximately ₹200, by an auto rickshaw to get to Madh Island from Malad station. Malad, a suburb in western Mumbai, remains one of the city's most crowded places to live in and is an important train station. What is not commonly discussed today is that the earliest dubbing studios were established in this suburb. In a strange sense, Malad has had a connection with Bollywood that is not often spoken of and yet there are a host of people who still claim to have seen a Dev Anand or an Ashok Kumar sitting in their large cars at the railway crossing.

To date, Madh Island remains a hot tourist destination with its beaches being a key attraction. In fact, the place is just several fishing villages that have come together. Television serials are shot on a regular basis here and a visit to Madh Island often provokes a warning from well-wishers who think the ill-tempered Aksa Beach is still strong enough to gobble up a few souls. The wealthy, of course, have sprawling properties here and some large hotels too are quite conspicuous.

When Chandra came to Madh Island a couple of months before shooting commenced for *Don*, he was pretty taken in

Nariman and Chandra at Madh Island. To Chandra's left is chief assistant director, Vijay Gosain

by the deceptive calm of the beach. He thought to himself that a couple of shots here could look nice given the vast expanse of the sea. A chase scene was just one of the thoughts that crossed his mind. A sequence from David Lean's *Ryan's Daughter* with the heroine walking in the sand with an umbrella was also an inspiration. He was convinced that the effect could be quite spectacular. Chandra was not entirely off the mark.

The first time the 'suitcase bomb' trick was filmed, it was for the opening sequence in *Don.* The script provided for another scene and Chandra was quite excited about it. If the first shot was filmed in an open tract of land, this one surely

Chandra and Amitabh at Madh Island discussing the suitcase bomb scene

needed to have a different look to it. Madh Island was already on the director's mind and he decided to film an important confrontation between Iftekhar and Don here. The 'suitcase bomb' would again be used and Amitabh would escape again. The scene involved a car chase as well and the beach seemed like a great place to start off.

As Amitabh's sleek car (foreign needless to say) makes its way to the beach, the hero scarcely imagines that he is going to be accosted by cops led by Iftekhar. In fact, a phone call is earlier intercepted by the police and that leads to this unpleasant surprise. A cool Amitabh walks towards Iftekhar and offers to hand over the money to him if he is allowed to get away. A furious Iftekhar reprimands him and it is at this point that Amitabh throws the suitcase in the air. It explodes before it hits the ground and that gives him just enough time to plan his escape. In the confusion that unexpectedly hits the cops, Amitabh gets away in a car that is not the one he drives in with. Funnily enough, the car that he escapes in is a somewhat battered one! After all, the limited budget could not have allowed for anything more luxurious than that.

This is the point where the chase begins, which remains quite a thrilling sequence for the background music and the hero's deft handling of his car. The reality was far from that. For one thing, it was quite a shock to Chandra that Iftekhar could not drive. The other problem was that filming of a car chase in the city was impossible to execute with the incessant traffic. Again, it was innovative direction that saved the day.

Due to Iftekhar's inability to be at the wheel, the camera was filmed in the reverse direction. However, this made it difficult to get Amitabh's car in the frame. It meant that there had to be roads and lanes that were not only free of traffic but had to be large enough to accommodate this little beast of a car. Chandra knew this shot had to be done in such a manner that the viewer would never figure out that something was not right.

The answer came in the form of a motorbike, belonging to A. Mansoor, the fight coordinator, that was lying around the sets. It was large enough to seat two and could move quite impressively. Chandra got Mansoor to ride the bike and he rode pillion. The improvisation was that Mansoor did not face the rider and sat with his back to him. Holding a camera in his hand, he instructed the young chap to move around Juhu as fast as he could. The camera just filmed the traffic that was actually coming towards the bike. When one watches it on the screen, it does seem like a car that is trying to get past the traffic smartly. Of course, there are shots of

Amitabh driving the car shot from various angles with the objective of making it as realistic as possible.

To say that there were constraints during the filming of *Don* would merely be stating the obvious. It was critical for Chandra to get past all of this. He wanted an international touch to the film but he had to make do with little money and, hence, look for locations in and around the city. If they looked international enough, it was great. If they did not, he just had to make do with what was available. In his mind, he knew one thing: *film se location banti hai* (the location is made by a film) and certainly not the other way round. Of course, he knew there was a little footage from the 1973 holiday in London which certainly could be used. He was waiting to surprise Nariman with that.

The scene where the street singer is shown footage of his lookalike who is now dead was shot in Waheeda Rehman's house. The lady was gracious enough to lend her living room for a day and, as the camera rolls, a smoking Iftekhar asks the street singer to take a good look at his more sophisticated lookalike. In Chandra's mind, this was the perfect moment to bring in the London footage.

A day before the shot was conceived, he went to Nariman with what he had filmed in London. 'Bawa, take a look at this. I think you will like it,' said Chandra quite earnestly. The pot-bellied cameraman was smitten by what he saw and took a moment to measure his words. 'Bachu, there is only one issue. Every shot filmed overseas needs government approval and we do not have that,' he said very calmly. A distraught Chandra knew there was no point arguing and did not manage to hide his disappointment. It was a lesson

Chandra and Amitabh at Hanging Gardens in Malabar Hill shooting an important scene

cruelly learnt for the young director that bureaucracy, more often than not, wins the day. The next time around, he would be a lot more cautious. Chandra still finds it hard to recollect where that footage of London lies. It would be worth a fortune in today's context.

The aforementioned sequence has Amitabh walking past various tall structures with a briefcase and chic sunglasses. He is well dressed and the gangster impression is well conveyed. He was supposed to be shown coming out of the London museum holding a newspaper that has a report of a big heist. Towards the end of that shot, he meets a lady who is also in sunglasses. It was filmed in Mumbai's upmarket Hanging Gardens. Chandra's sister, Sudha, who had already hosted the Bachchan couple in London during the honeymoon, sportingly agreed to be the lady handing over the briefcase to the hero.

There was more of the Barot family connection in the film, though not all of it was planned. When Pran is out of jail, he walks past a school where his two children are playing football. The man is oblivious to the rest of his surroundings and, as the ball lands close to him, he just throws it back inside. That school is Sacred Hearts and is located at Santacruz in western Mumbai. As Chandra was to realize many years later, his wife, Deepa, was a student there when that shot was being filmed. To this day, Deepa recalls the buzz in the school when the football scene was shot.

One thing that Chandra has not ever let go of over the years has been his love for the camera. And one is not referring to the movie camera. Chandra is constantly clicking pictures of events, monuments or pretty much anything and everything that he finds interesting. In Mumbai, one sight that always caught his fancy was the Dhobi Ghat in Mahalaxmi. It is a fascinating sight where clothes from the city's hotels and hospitals are washed and dried in the open. It is a manual operation with hordes of washers working with a flogging stone.

Chandra and Amitabh during the Dhobi Ghat sequence

In the second half of the film, Amitabh is constantly on the run as he is chased relentlessly by the cops. Chandra told Amitabh what he had in mind and they met the following day outside the Dhobi Ghat. 'Tiger, this is a straightforward shot. You have to run as if you are being chased,' was the brief from the director to the attentive star. Amitabh did exactly that and the washers, who had no idea there was a film being shot, were taken unaware by the presence of the star. That probably explains the somewhat perplexed look on their faces. The entire sequence was filmed in an hour. The shot of Amitabh running became the iconic image for the poster of *Don* and is often accompanied by Zeenat holding a pistol.

Chandra began shooting that sequence in the Dhobi Ghat, but completed it at the Chandivali studios. Here the shot has

Chandra and Amitabh shooting a key scene on the Mumbai–Ahmedabad highway

Amitabh moving the clothes to get a better view of the road and trying to confuse the cops who are in hot pursuit.

There were a couple of shots that were filmed on the

Mumbai–Ahmedabad highway that remain integral to the film. For instance, Amitabh spraying petrol on Iftekhar is one shot which required a lot of open space. This scene leads to the hero regaining his memory, leading to another twist in the tale. The shot of Amitabh standing on a bridge lighting a cigarette is also on the same highway. It has Iftekhar standing below as the hero chats very casually with the man who has planted him on this dreaded mission.

There was a need for a karate instructor for *Don* and Chandra was quite clear that the person best suited for it was Jairaj. Viewers will find it hard to forget Jairaj who plays Dayal Uncle, the judo instructor. It is to Jairaj Zeenat comes after her brother has been killed by Don. By the time *Don* was released, Jairaj was already in his late sixties. In fact, he was already a big name in the Hindi film industry by then having made his debut in films as far back as 1930.

Even in the 1970s, Jairaj had one of the best physiques in the industry. During the early part of his career, he worked with the best names like V. Shantaram, Motilal, Prithviraj Kapoor, Nirupa Roy and Meena Kumari. Jairaj had come to Mumbai from Hyderabad where he had studied in the city's prestigious Nizam's College. He made his mark in the industry over time and was seen in films like *Baharon Ke Sapne*, *Neel Kamal* and even *Sholay*. By the time Jairaj, a Telugu by birth, died in 2000, he had starred in over 170 films and was a recipient of the Dadasaheb Phalke Award.

Chandra shot the introduction scene between Jairaj and Zeenat at the Talwalkars gym on Peddar Road. To say the young director was in awe of the well-built Jairaj would not be an exaggeration. For his part, the man with the dream physique was modest and had no airs at all. He had seen many generations pass by during his long stint in the industry. Talwalkars has today made way for a rather plush building where the Jindal group has its headquarters. Both Chandra and Jairaj were quite amused when people, for years after the release of *Don,* asked them the same question: *Aapka gym kahan par hai?* Where is your gym?

The search for a location for each scene in *Don* was almost an obsession for Chandra. One evening, as he was driving past Bandra's famed reclamation, he was taken in by the crowd at a circus. There were hordes of people lining up to get tickets for the next show. In almost no time, Nariman and

Pran with the circus owner

he spoke to the owner of the circus to seek time for a shoot. Eventually, the scene with Pran in the circus was filmed there. A closer look at the film will reveal that this was not the only part of the film which showed Bandra.

The suburb in those days had some elegant colonial structures and that, with the vast greenery, was very attractive. When Om Shivpuri walks with Iftekhar and Satyen Kappu towards his car in one of the opening scenes, he is intrigued by Satyen's expensive watch. Sensing that the situation could get out of control, Satyen quickly says that the watch was gifted to him by a friend. This was filmed in one of those colonial bungalows where the owner gladly loaned it to the crew for a couple of hours. Interestingly, the bungalow was barely a few yards away from a structure that would house a very famous occupant in the time to come.

When *Don* was being filmed, Shah Rukh Khan was still a diligent student and an enthusiastic stage actor at Delhi's St. Columba's School. The thought of an Amitabh film being released a few years later, or the possibility of him starring in its remake, was clearly not a part of his daily curriculum. For that matter, he could well have laughed if someone had told him he would live in a sprawling bungalow in Bandra at the turn of the century.

Nariman's office was also in Bandra and was very close to Mehboob Studios. He was quite amused when Chandra filmed the scene where Amitabh drops the letter in Satyen's house in the second half since the Nariman Films' board had to be removed for that shoot. This was not the only piece of minor improvisation in *Don*. Even for the rather treacherous 'upar se neeche' shot, Amitabh's prime objective is to hand over the tell-all diary to Iftekhar. Miraculously, the diary is neatly packed in a plastic cover which was a bit of a last minute insertion after it was realized that the actor was going to fall into a swimming pool. Quite amusingly, Iftekhar does not fail to make a mention of that in his brief conversation with Amitabh.

Getting the film to look seamless was going to be a hard task but Chandra knew that he had very little choice on that one. Given that the scenes were shot in studios, people's houses, highways and even in a washers' corner, the only way to keep the audience occupied was a tight script. The fact is *Don* did not fall short on that which certainly made life easy for this young, promising director. If scenes were shot in familiar locations, he did his bit to make sure that they looked different in his film.

One instance was Om Shivpuri's hideout which is shown in full splendour towards the end of the film. The living room

Amitabh and Zeenat in the graveyard scene

has Om, Zeenat and several members of the gang talking just as Pran makes his entry. This is the same bungalow where Yash Chopra shot the famous confrontation scene between the two brothers in *Deewar* and it is indeed the one that Amitabh proudly shows Nirupa Roy in the same film as an indication of his new-found prosperity.

When it came to shooting the climax, Chandra was anything but perturbed. He needed a graveyard and the one in Dadar was perfect. This is the scene when Om's real identity is uncovered to the police and the tell-all diary just keeps flying from one side to the other. Again, it was Nariman's counsel that prevailed.

When Chandra went to Nariman with the idea of shooting in the Dadar graveyard, it found no favour with the cameraman. 'Bachu, I think this is avoidable. It is too sensitive to shoot on people's graves,' he said quite tersely. The only option was to create a graveyard but since it was the climax, Chandra knew it just had to be done.

The obvious choice was Desh Mukherjee, one of the most well-known art directors. The man had already worked on films like *Mera Saaya* and *Teesri Kasam*. Chandra was with him in *Purab Aur Paschim*, *Shor* and the more recent *Roti, Kapada Aur Makaan*. Interestingly, Desh was directing *Immaan Dharam* with Amitabh, Rekha, Shashi and Sanjeev.

When Nariman and Chandra asked Desh for help, the answer was in the affirmative. All the art director asked for was time. 'Chandra, I will need twenty-one days to design a graveyard,' was his request. Chandra said yes and was quietly confident that it would look real. And it did.

When Chandra and his crew descended on Chandivali studios to film the climax, what they saw was the work of a professional. He thanked Desh profusely and immediately got down to filming the scene. There was just one problem. The set had graves without any names. Immediately, Chandra decided that the names of the people who formed the crew of *Don* was the best option. That's precisely what took place and a close look at the scene will reveal names like Alfred Francis, Joe D'Souza, Felix J. Braganza and Leo Gomes. Some of these names also appear in the titles of *Don*. For instance, Joe D'Souza was the operative cameraman.

Ingenuity again took over when a taxi shell was doused with tar and petrol and set on fire. It is this shell into which the diary is flung. What came as a pleasant surprise was the extent to which kids loved this part of the climax. Full of twists and turns, coupled with incredibly appropriate music, the kids just loved it and could not have enough of it. A huge plus was that Amitabh had established his sense of timing as a comic artist with films like *Amar, Akbar, Anthony* and the climax here was him at his funniest. The only problem was

Amitabh in the graveyard scene

that the star had dislocated his shoulder after a fall and was in some pain. Jaya was calling him time and again to check if all was well. Luckily, none of that pain shows in the sequence.

For Chandra, there was an unexpected story that was building up. Nariman's health was not in the best shape and his blood sugar was looking a little alarming. Chandra did not realize the magnitude of what was to unfold shortly. It would prove to be a life-changing experience.

CHAPTER ELEVEN

In the mid-1970s, the Emergency brought with it censorship in various forms. From June 1975, the situation was such that the press, radio or cinema or for that matter broadcasting, in any form, would be regulated by the government. No questions could be asked and those in the business just had to fall in line.

The tremors were already being felt in the film industry. Gulzar's *Aandhi* had run into a bit of an issue since it was felt that the lead character bore an uncanny resemblance to Indira Gandhi. It was after considerable discussion and negotiation that the film finally hit the theatres. *Kissa Kursi Ka* was not so lucky and this political satire, starring Shabana Azmi and Raj Babbar, did not see the light of day even after it was cleared with forty cuts.

A month after the Emergency was declared, Indira Gandhi reached out to Manoj Kumar to make a film called *Naya Bharat*. This would be around the Emergency and Manoj said yes on the condition that Mrs Gandhi made a personal appearance in the film. Salim–Javed were to write the dialogues. 'Amitabh, too, agreed to be a part of it,' recalls Manoj. Sanjay

Gandhi had other ideas and was not comfortable about his mother in the film. 'You will have to settle for a duplicate,' he told Manoj. The project was later shelved.

It was not just films that suffered during this period. Well-known personalities too faced the heat and there was very little that they could do. Shatrughan Sinha and Kishore Kumar were not in the Congress' good books for a host of reasons and they paid a pretty hefty price. While the actor's films were banned by the government during the period, the legendary singer's voice would not be heard on All India Radio or Doordarshan. The somewhat adventurous bunch like Dev Anand and I.S. Johar took the decision to launch the National Party which, over time, faded into oblivion.

Filmmakers were not a happy bunch. When Amitabh returned to Mumbai after a brief trip to Delhi, the news was not good. Chandra was stunned when he heard that the government stipulated that only 90 feet of film would be permitted for fight sequences. The director had a pretty grand vision of a blood-filled fight between Amitabh and Shetty. That was not the big concern. Instead, the worry was about dealing with the all-important climax.

In private, Chandra had decided that his film would have shades of *The Godfather*, with villains relentlessly firing their guns. Ever since he had watched the film with Amitabh in London, the word 'gruesome', for some reason, had stuck in his head. *Don* was a film where the script allowed this kind of violence and he was looking forward to shooting such scenes. The censorship now meant that some key scenes, including the climax, would be severely diluted. Simply put, the climax had to be changed with the red diary now becoming the most important component.

It is worth noting that the first killing in the film takes place

Chandra with Amitabh on the sets of *Don*

just after the titles. When Amitabh decides to kill the police informer, he says, '*Mujhe iske joothe acche nahin lage*' (I didn't like his shoes) with nonchalance. The plan was to show some blood there to establish the fact that Amitabh, in this form, was really wicked. What was eventually shot made an impact, though it would have been more hard-hitting if the director could have gone ahead with what he had in mind. There are more instances of censorship like the scene in which Amitabh, as the taxi driver, knocks off Ramesh. There was no blood here again and what goes unnoticed is that it was Chandra at the wheel and not the hero. Of course, once the street singer enters the picture, he does not even hold a gun.

There were a couple of more instances where the script had to be adjusted. In the confrontation between Shetty and Amitabh in the villain's house, the liquor bottle is broken though there is no blood to be seen. The only liberty that was taken was in the scene where the police discover the corpse of Don. Shot in Vasai Fort or Bassein Fort, which is a little more than an hour from south Mumbai by train, this scene had to show some trace of Don having been shot. Chandra decided to use an expensive face mask that he had picked up during one of his visits to London. Without a doubt, Chandra would have loved to have had the quintessential Western look in these sequences. He chose to err on the side of caution and that, in the circumstances, seemed like a practical thing to do.

The diary in *Don* is the part that keeps the film together. It is first exposed to the viewer when Kamal Kapoor and Amitabh open the safe vault. A slightly intrigued Amitabh browses through the diary and even if he realizes how potent the information in it is, he does not let it show. Subsequently, it is smartly picked up by the street singer without the knowledge of the gang and the rest of the plot then just moves on briskly. Then it lands in Iftekhar's hands before it reaches Pran. For the hero, it remains the elusive object that alone can prove his innocence. Even in the climax, it comes down to the ability to grab the diary (and the right one!) at any cost that makes the sequence so absorbing.

The role of the diary in the film became far more important than what was planned once it was clear that there would be virtually no violence. For Chandra, it was a bit of a compromise from the creative point of view and he quickly decided that he would make do with what he had. If the diary could be used smartly, then that was the way the film was going to be shot.

The inspiration for the diary came from the 1969 English film *If It's Tuesday, This Must Be Belgium.* Here, the theme revolved around an eighteen days' bus trip from London to Rome, with most of the passengers being first-time visitors to Europe. The film had a sequence where a diary is used.

Amitabh in the climax sequence of *Don*

Chandra, who by then was already watching a film a night, was taken in by the concept of the diary.

There were very few people in the Hindi film industry who were not enamoured by the diary sequence in *Don* and it was often the subject discussed at big filmi parties those days. One such instance was a lavish evening that was held in Dilip Kumar's palatial Bandra bungalow in early 1979. This was in honour of the well-known Kannada actor, Dr Rajkumar, who was visiting Mumbai. The city's film fraternity turned up in large numbers and the conversation effortlessly went into the early hours.

G.P. Sippy, a much loved man, was one of the attendees that night. His production, *Shaan*, was in the making and it would be released towards the end of the following year. If Sippy had hit it big with *Sholay*, the film's massive ₹3 crore budget had given him many a sleepless night. At the party, an animated Sippy was talking to Dilip and Gulshan Rai, the producer whose banner, Trimurti Films, had already released *Johny Mera Naam*, *Deewar* and *Trishul*. The moment he spotted Chandra, he called out to the young man. Placing his arm around Chandra's shoulders, he told the other gentlemen that he had spent ₹10 lakh on one train sequence shot in *Sholay*. '*Aur yahaan par Chandra ne dus rupaiye ki laal diary mein picture ka climax kar diya*, (And here, Chandra filmed the climax using a diary for ten rupees)' said Sippy as the others burst out laughing. Chandra just smiled and did not say very much. Only he was aware of the sweat and toil that went into the making of *Don*. 'What if this film had flopped?' he wondered to himself before he was engrossed in another entertaining conversation with Dilip.

CHAPTER TWELVE

The real Interpol officer in *Don* does make a fleeting appearance in the film. Viewers would probably struggle to recall the presence of Pinchoo Kapoor, the burly actor who has a slight argument with Om Shivpuri towards the end of the film. Pinchoo was seen in a few films for about two decades in the 1970s and 1980s like *Imman Dharam* and *Bidaai*, though it was the character of R.K. Malik in Chandra's film that got him more recognition.

If things had gone according to the plan, Farida Jalal would also have been a part of *Don* in a five-minute all-important appearance. The bubbly actress, who had already made a mark in *Aradhana* as Rajesh Khanna's girlfriend, knew Nariman since she had starred in the ill-fated *Zindagi Zindagi*. Nariman took a special liking to this young lady who was very impressive in *Majboor* as Amitabh's sister and also in Gulzar's 1975 release, *Khushboo*. It was on Nariman's recommendation that Farida was roped in for *Don*, where she would play Pinchoo's daughter.

The scene was set to be filmed at Santacruz airport in Mumbai, where Farida would get off the flight and greet

Pinchoo warmly. The build-up to this scene was perfect, with Om threatening Farida that Pinchoo would be killed if she acted funny. Importantly, Satyen Kappu, by this time in the film, is a little uneasy about Om and thinks there is more to this smooth talking Interpol officer. He decides to keep an eye on Om and follows him to the airport. The moment Farida sees Om, she says, 'Hi Daddy' quite casually and hugs him affectionately. A slightly confused Satyen watches this drama unfold and just shrugs his shoulders before walking away.

At the post-production stage, it was decided to delete this scene. The consensus between the director and his talented duo of writers was that this was not helping the script. While it was not an easy decision, it also showed the extent to which the commitment to make *Don* a tight film was always the focus. Over time, Farida would establish herself as an actress of immense talent with remarkable performances in films like *Shatranj Ke Khiladi*, *Pushpak*, *Mammo*, *Dilwale Dulhania Le Jayenge*, *Dil To Pagal Hai*, *Kuch Kuch Hota Hai* and *Kabhi Kushi Kabhie Gham*.

If Farida could count herself a little unlucky, Amitabh too was not let off that easily. The young man was quite furious about being stuck with one outfit through most of the second half. The argument put forth was that he was on the run and there was really no place for a change in outfit. Wisely, it was decided to stick to the script and not make any changes.

In the scene where the on-the-run Amitabh meets Zeenat in a restaurant (Caesars Palace in Bandra with some loud music playing in the background), he tells her to pick up some clothes for him. The deal is that he will meet her at Mahalaxmi Station a week later where he will take the new set of clothes from her. When this proposal went to Salim–Javed, it was rejected outright. The duo said that they would not change the script under any circumstances. It is hard to guess if they imagined how iconic that outfit of the on-the-run Amitabh would become in the mind of the viewer for years to come.

The unexpected mention of Sanjeev Kumar, early in the film, is pretty interesting too. Barring the extent to which the accomplished actor's character in *Naya Din Nai Raat* was so impressive that it was enough to get Chandra to use it in *Don*, Sanjeev was never planned to be a part of *Don*. Again, it was the talented writers who came up with the smart idea to get Iftekhar to mention his name in passing. When Om meets the police crew just after the titles to brief them on the treacherous assignment ahead, it is Iftekhar who rattles off the names of gangsters like Shyam Narang, Don and a certain Haribhai Jariwala, which was actually Sanjeev's real name.

Hailing from a conservative Gujarati family, Sanjeev made his debut in *Hum Hindustani*, before establishing himself with intense performances in *Khilona* and *Sunghursh*. In the mid-1970s, he was unforgettable in films like *Sholay*, *Aandhi* and *Mausam*. Sadly, Haribhai Jariwala never appears in Don and is restricted to a casual mention in the early part of the film. It is commonly known that Gujaratis often adopt the professions they came from as their surnames as well. Going by that logic, Sanjeev should have come from a family of jariwallahs. Surely, this was one loss for that enterprising community that Bollywood accepted gleefully. By the time Sanjeev passed away somewhat unexpectedly in 1985 at a relatively young age of forty-seven, he was, beyond doubt, one of the finest actors who would ever grace the screen. *Don* could well be the only instance where Sanjeev is ever mentioned by his real name.

Never once did Chandra forget that he was a novice in the presence of stars. The good part though was that this never came in the way of working and every artist put his/her best foot forward. This actually made it easy for Chandra to experiment as a debut director and his opinions were always taken well.

In the case of Om, it was critical to establish in the actor's mind that he was not the real Interpol officer but the big boss of a gang at large. To the audience, however, Om's real identity is the actual twist in the climax. Chandra, for his part, told Om very clearly that he would have to think for a second before saying anything. The rationale for this was simple. Om would have to think to himself what the real Interpol officer would have done in a certain situation. He would then decide what to say.

This attention to detail stands out in the scene where Iftekhar

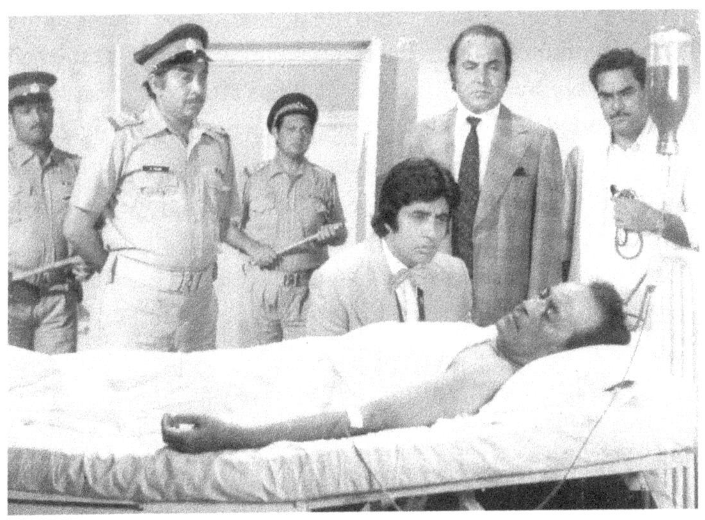

Amitabh with Iftekhar, Satyen Kappu and Om Shivpuri watching the cop dying

is in the hospital after being critically shot. As Amitabh tries to prove his innocence, Satyen and Om are keeping close tabs on the hero. A frantic Amitabh implores Iftekhar to tell everyone that he is nothing but a street singer. At that moment, the panic on Om's face is telling, though the audience is too caught up with Amitabh's situation to really notice anything else.

Chandra's directorial skill is apparent throughout the movie like the scene where Shetty is repeatedly taunted by Amitabh in the police van. Here, the brief to Shetty was simple. 'I want you to sport the Dilip Kumar killer look,' was all Chandra said to the villain. As the van sways from one side to another, which was the result of people shaking the van from outside, Shetty snarls at Amitabh and finally snaps after the hero spits on him.

Again, when Helen is in the midst of luring Amitabh into the 'Yeh Mera Dil' song, the hero quite wickedly asks for her name. This is after the two of them have spent some intimate time together in a hotel room. Chandra has asked Helen to say Sonia a little musically to give an indication to the audience that a song lay ahead. Of course, Helen's name in the film is Kamini as viewers will remember.

When it came to Kamal Kapoor, Chandra was smitten by the man's eyes and knew they could do all the talking. His introduction in the film is in the '*Mujhe iske joothe acche nahin lage*' scene where he is agitated about Amitabh having killed a person called Rajesh. In one part of that scene, he turns his head gently to his left where Amitabh is standing to give him a good, hard look. Kamal does not say very much and it is the look that says it all. His soft-spoken but hard demeanour would stand out in most of his films. *Don*, where he was the cool Narang with his well-oiled hair slickly combed backwards, was no exception.

CHAPTER THIRTEEN

What was not completely planned during the making of *Don* was the attention to even the smallest of characters. Insignificant, as they seem in the film, there is no getting away from the fact that they would be remembered in some form for many years to come. Be it Jairaj, Pinchoo Kapoor or the three thugs who confront Don in the first scene, they all have a place in the film. There were others as well without whom the film may not have been discussed the way it is even after so many years.

Macmohan, who is still remembered for that solitary line in *Sholay* where he plays Sambha, was one such character. In *Don*, like many other films that came before or after, he was called just Mac. In reality, Mohan Makijany made his debut in the mid-1960s and, over time, was seen in films like *Heera Panna*, *Zanjeer*, *Manoranjan* and *Majboor*. The scene following the titles is when Mac is first introduced in the film. He is the one who is gently reprimanded by Don after the police informer, Rajesh, has been killed.

Interestingly enough, a lot of directors decided to have Macmohan as their lucky mascot and that explains his presence in multi-starrers like *Sholay* and *Shaan*. He was Chandra's good friend and his presence in *Don*, although not insignificant, should not to be taken for granted. The scenes where Mac quite foolishly points a loaded pistol at the handicapped Pran towards the end in Om's presence is quite comical. So is the line soon after when Pran refers to Mac's bearded look quite sarcastically. When *Don* was being made, Mac was already in his forties and was seen on the big screen until his death in 2010. The lanky man with the beard was also Raveena Tandon's uncle.

The mention of the name Sebisco (or Zebisco to some) brings back memories of that fair, well-built man who beats up Amitabh after the 'My Name is Anthony Gonsalves' song in *Amar Akbar Anthony*. Fondly called Hercules in Bollywood, Yusuf Khan was from Hyderabad and was the envy of most people for being remarkably muscular. He was Parveen's bodyguard in *Amar Akbar Anthony* and was Vikram in *Don*. He is the one who is constantly with the hero, and in his tight jeans and somewhat one-size-small T-shirt, he does not spare a chance to flash his physique.

There were not very many in Bollywood who could have beaten Iftekhar as the cop. Jagdish Raj was up there and it is claimed that he donned the khaki outfit in almost 150 films. That fact found him a place in the Guinness Book of World Records. Unlike Iftekhar, Jagdish would have just a handful of dialogues in any film and was seen rather than heard. He was in Yash Chopra's *Ittefaq* and also in *Johny Mera Naam*. In *Deewar*, he played Jaggi, the baddie, who is given the job of killing Amitabh. In *Don*, he plays a stage artist who impersonates a cop with the task of firing blank bullets at Zeenat. Jagdish was a regular in films in the 1970s and in the following decade as well. His daughter, Anita Raj, too made a reasonable mark in Bollywood as an actress.

Alankar Joshi, known more popularly as Master Alankar, starred in films like *Andaz, Seeta Aur Geeta, Khhotte Sikkay, Majboor, Deewar* and *Sholay* before *Don* was released. By Chandra's own confession, Alankar, who was Pallavi Joshi's brother, did not have to be told what to do. He had already worked with the likes of Ramesh Sippy and Yash Chopra before signing up with the first-time director. In the role of Deepu with his sister, Munni, played by a new entrant, Baby Bilkish, *Don* was a film where Alankar had a meaty role all the way to the climax.

The role of the duplicates in *Don* was no less significant and Chandra zeroed in on the tried and tested Manik Irani. Being tall, he was the perfect fit for Amitabh. Manik was a regular in a host of films that Manmohan Desai and Prakash Mehra directed, where he regularly played the 'other Amitabh'.

In *Don,* he is the one who runs from the police at Mahalaxmi Station and jumps off the bridge. It is again Manik who is looking to get on to the running train as Iftekhar attempts to get him in that famous chase sequence. Of course, his presence was absolutely critical in the climax where the diary is moving from one end of the graveyard to the other.

For Zeenat, given that there were so many stunt scenes, Hussain, another well-known stunt artist was chosen. Viewers would recall how Zeenat's hairstyle changes in the film in line with what is required and Hussain too, as a result, had to change looks. It was really the case of a male stunt artist with or without the wig. Like Manik, Hussain was a key component in the climax.

Pran with his duplicate on the sets of *Don*

For most directors, duplicates are as important as the stars and should also possess the abilities of professional fighters. They have to be agile and can scarcely afford to make a mistake. It is actually these stunt artists who reinforce the belief in the minds of the viewer that the hero is invincible.

While Chandra used a male for Zeenat, he used a lady for Pran. The actor's role required him to play the trapeze artist in a circus to support an ailing wife and two little children. Once tragedy befalls him, he goes to jail and the sole aim after that is to finish Iftekhar, the cop who shot him in the leg. The role required a competent circus performer to display his craft for a living and, later in the film, the character uses the very same rope trick to get away from Om's gang. For that particular escape scene, Chandra decided to get in special effects to create an array of colours to light up the screen.

He immediately contacted Ramesh Meer, who was already working with Manmohan Desai on films like *Amar Akbar Anthony* and *Dharam Veer*. A product of the Film & Television Institute of India in Pune, Ramesh, a special effects brain, realized that he had a pretty serious job on hand. Digging into his reservoir of talent, he employed the matte technique in filmmaking where two or more visual elements are combined to form one final image.

In this case, the entire set, which was housed in Mehboob Studios, was painted in blue. Ramesh then made models of buildings and people moving around since the shot required Pran to walk across the rope from one building to the other. The shot of Pran on the rope was filmed in complete darkness and the actor was in reality walking barely four feet above the ground holding his two children. Eventually, the two images of Pran on the rope and the set in blue were merged.

The entire sequence was shot in three days. Ramesh would go on to do the special effects for films like *Pardes* and *Hum Dil De Chuke Sanam*.

In this day and age, that shot may look tacky. What needs to be understood is that this was filmed at a time when special effects as a concept was unknown to most people in the film industry. It was a period of experimentation and being inspired by what one saw in Hollywood. As the set at Mehboob Studios was being painted blue, Chandra had an unexpected visitor.

Subhash Ghai was in the midst of his directorial debut, *Kalicharan*, that starred Shatrughan Sinha and Reena Roy. Word about the matte technique had spread and Subhash dropped in to see for himself what the buzz was all about. He was, not surprisingly, taken in by what he saw.

Photographer Bernie Abramson with Zeenat on the sets of *Don*. He was visiting India then

Pran with Nariman on the sets of *Don*

For a good part of *Don*, Pran was in his all-black outfit. This stood out in the scene where Ramesh was called in (the scene with Pran and the two children). For the incredibly talented actor, this role was quite different from what he had done in the past. He often told Chandra that he had rediscovered the joy of acting in the 1970s when he quietly bid goodbye to the bad man.

Be it in *Bobby*, *Zanjeer*, *Amar Akbar Anthony* or *Don*, he was playing roles that were a far cry from his villainous past. He was very comfortable with Chandra and knew him from the time he had worked with Manoj Kumar. Being the cynical and frustrated JJ (Jasjit as he is called on a couple of occasions) in *Don* was a role he worked on religiously. Pran was known to be a man of dignity and etiquette and when he spoke to Amitabh, it was Amitji, though it was more informal with

Chandra whom he called Chander. The industry referred to him as Pran saab.

Pran was so passionate about his craft that he had paintings of all the characters he had played. It is estimated that he starred in over 350 films. Another fetish of his was wigs and he loved to sport a different look in every film. In more ways than one, that has been copied by Gulshan Grover. Pran had an astonishing memory and regaled the crew of *Don* with some unforgettable anecdotes from the past.

Chandra knew Pran was a stickler for time. Given his own ability to party late, he was always aware that this actor

A still from the scene in *Don* where Amitabh and Pran fight it out over the kids with the wall in the background

would be ready with his make-up at 9.30 a.m. sharp. He was a director's actor and never drifted from the script. For the shot where Pran is trying to protect his kids from Amitabh in a case of a mistaken identity, Chandra realized the scene written by Salim-Javed needed such a narrow lane that was impossible to find. A wall was soon constructed by Desh Mukherjee in Mehboob Studios. Here, Pran stands in the middle with his hand on one side and the walking stick on the other. The wall was created in almost no time.

Pran was such an established star that by the time *Don* was in the making, he commanded twice as much respect as Amitabh. After *Zanjeer, Majboor* and *Amar Akbar Anthony*, Amitabh and Pran were a comfortable duo. They would be seen together again in films like *Kaalia* and *Sharaabi.*

In the film, Pran's all-black outfit came from Kachins, a name that was already being associated with some of the biggest stars in Bollywood. Amitabh's wardrobe too came from there. Interestingly enough, his special costume designer for the film was his sister-in-law, Ramola Bachchan, whose name finds a mention in the titles as well. This was not the only instance she performed this role. She was also involved in Manmohan Desai's 1979 release, *Suhaag*. Of course, *Suhaag* became one of the biggest grossers of that year.

Chandra was clear that his hero would be dressed immaculately and the items that had been picked up in London during Amitabh's honeymoon with Jaya came in handy. For a good part of the film, the gangster and his lookalike are attired in a smart bow tie that go well with eye-pleasing colours like grey and beige for the coat and bell bottomed trousers, which were a rage in the 1970s.

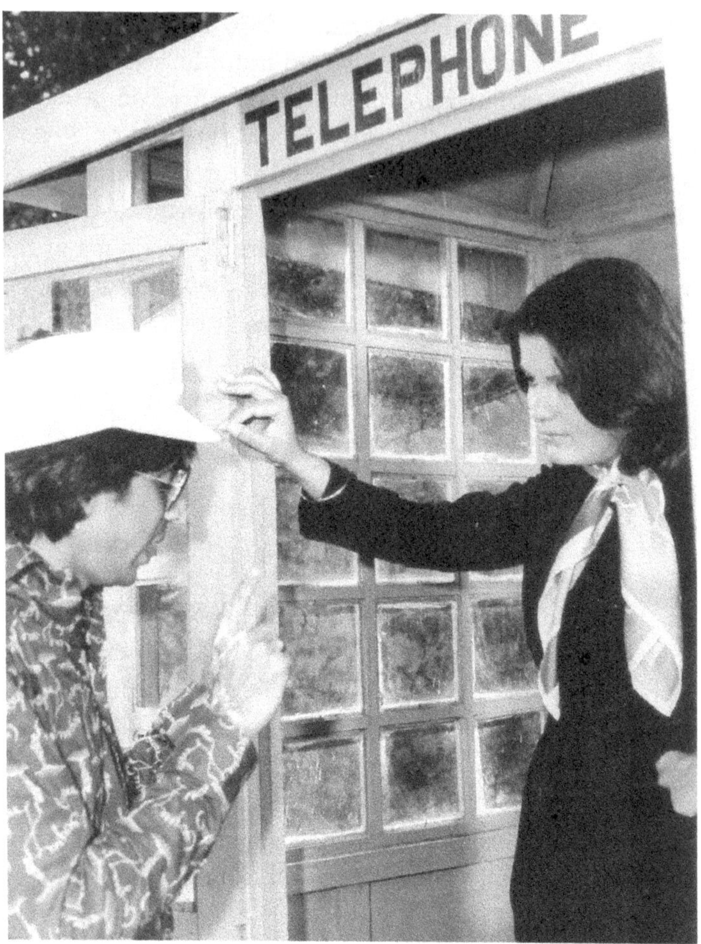

Chandra directing Zeenat

His personal sunglasses were used quite extensively in the outdoor sequences.

To this day, Chandra insists that there was no specific budget for costumes and the film was shot with what was easily and readily available. For Zeenat, he turned to Mani

Rabadi, who was already a name in the costume designing world. Mani, who was Shammi Aunty's sister, was initially noticed for designing Mala Sinha's outfits in the 1966 release *Dillagi*. She would make her mark in films like *An Evening in Paris*, *Prince*, *Naya Zamana*, *Roti Kapada Aur Makaan* and *Hum Kisi Se Kum Naheen* and also for Madhuri Dixit in *Hum Aapke Hain Koun*.

Zeenat had a casual, cool look in *Don* and she wore Western outfits throughout the film. It was either the long skirt or the more casual T-shirt. She was the modern day heroine and Mani did not have too much of a problem designing any of her outfits.

Chandra was clear that his hero would have to look elegant with a touch of aristocracy which his heroine needed to complement. He was already proud of the way his film looked. Little did he realize that a fatal turn of events was still waiting to play out. It was a telephone call that gave him the tragic news. It would take years for Chandra to recover from that blow.

CHAPTER FOURTEEN

The residents of Mumbai were in for an unexpected bout of heavy rain in November 1977. It was at least two months since the city's monsoon had bid its goodbye. Even those who had spent decades in the city were a trifle perplexed. The irony was that the city was in the midst of its famed second summer and this downpour meant that the umbrellas and raincoats had to be pulled out at least six months before they were needed.

This did not deter the city's film fraternity that was already in the midst of some serious work. The year, so far, had been pretty good with films like *Amar Akbar Anthony*, *Dharam Veer* and *Hum Kisi Se Kum Naheen* striking it big at the box-office. Manoj Kumar was working on his next big project for which shooting was already underway. Titled *Kranti*, the film starred Dilip, Shashi, Hema, Shatrughan, Parveen and, of course, Manoj. In film circles, it was already rumoured that *Kranti*, being written by Salim–Javed, would have a budget well in excess of ₹2 crore. Since it was the first film from the Manoj camp after *Roti Kapda Aur Makaan* in 1974, there was some serious interest building up.

On that day, Manoj was shooting in the city's Rajkamal Studio. Located in central Mumbai's densely populated Parel, the studio was owned by V. Shantaram, the name behind legendary films like *Jhanak Jhanak Payal Baje, Do Aankhen Barah Haath* and Jeetendra's debut project, *Geet Gaya Patharon Ne*. Then in his seventies, the veteran filmmaker had taken a bit of a backseat and his studio was being used quite extensively by Bollywood's finest names.

Looking at the incessant rainfall, Manoj was worried and wondered how he would film some of his key outdoor scenes. He let the thought pass as someone from his crew said the next shot could be filmed in a few minutes. As Manoj moved towards the camera, his eye was moving a little restlessly towards the adjoining wall that was looking a little flimsy. It had some deep cracks and could do with help.

Just at that very moment, the wall collapsed and the people on the sets were stunned by the loud noise. Before Manoj realized what was going on, a large chunk of the wall had landed on Nariman's hip. The gentle Parsi, who was the cameraman for *Kranti*, was in acute pain and it was clear that he had to be rushed to the hospital. Manoj was panic-stricken and was scouting for the nearest telephone. He had to convey the news to Chandra.

There was a moment of stunned silence when the news of Nariman's hip being injured reached Chandra. He just hoped nothing untoward had taken place and reached out to anyone he knew for access to the best doctors. Meanwhile, Nariman's wife, Salma, and their three children were really worried.

In almost no time, Nariman was admitted to the Bombay Hospital. It was one of the best known hospitals and Chandra was assured by family and well-wishers that it had the finest hip surgery specialists. The name of Dr K.T. Dholakia was one that was highly recommended.

Nariman, Amitabh and Chandra on the sets of *Don*

Soon, Nariman's family, Manoj and Chandra sought time with Dholakia. The doctor was a picture of assurance and said the hip replacement surgery could be done in ten days. The process was simple and only an artificial hip would need to be placed. Meanwhile, Manoj, who was in touch with some of his friends abroad, was told that homeopathy could be another option. That was considered to be risky and it was decided that the artificial hip was the best solution in the circumstance.

There was one serious problem though. For years, Nariman's sugar levels had remained high and Chandra was quite aware of that. He also knew diabetes had a tendency to complicate an existing problem and he hoped Nariman's body could hold out. This thought kept him occupied as Nariman was moved to the operation theatre in a couple of days.

The cameraman was in the hospital for about ten days and there was not a moment when Chandra was not close by. The young director's focus was only on how quickly his producer would recover. After all, there was precisely one scene that was left to be shot and the background score was to be recorded for *Don* and it required just a couple of days to wrap these up.

There was not much to be done in the hospital and Chandra was preoccupied with the doctors and Nariman's family. He could not wait for the jovial Parsi to recover and get back to being on the sets with him. Every time he looked at Nariman on the hospital bed, Chandra remembered the reprimand that was uttered incessantly on the sets of *Don*. 'Do not try to be Manoj Kumar,' said Nariman on the very first day of shooting. 'Yeh Mera Dil' was being filmed and the producer was convinced that his young protégé needed to get the Manoj hangover out of his system.

Yes, Chandra was a little hurt and he made it a point to do one thing each time a sequence was filmed. Mentally, he would visualize how his mentor would have shot it and he then would do something totally different. It had worked like a charm through the making of *Don* and Chandra knew deep down that the film looked nice. Whether it would work with the audience was not his immediate concern.

As the film's shooting was drawing to a close, Chandra knew there had to be the Manoj chhaap, his mark, somewhere

Chandra directing Zeenat

in the film. He decided to have this just before the climax in the graveyard. Om's real identity is now known to Amitabh and there is a sense of panic in the gang. At this juncture, Pran, quite unexpectedly, makes his way to Om's bungalow and asks for a hefty price for the red diary to be handed over. A cornered Om gives in and says Zeenat will meet Pran at the graveyard.

Just as Zeenat disappears, Om has a quiet conversation with his gang and asks them to keep an eye on the lady and Pran. The final command is to kill both of them once the diary is obtained. For this sequence, Chandra decided to film it the way Manoj might have. The camera was placed on the floor and the conversation between Om and his boys is filmed through a glass table. As the gang members—Macmohan and Kamal Kapoor among others—move closer to Om, the scene ends. Just before Nariman began rolling his camera, Chandra said, 'This scene is a tribute to Manoj Kumar.' At the end of that shot, Nariman and Chandra smiled warmly at each other. The pupil had had his way and the teacher was amused.

The joy of watching *Don* being released and the accompanying relief about extricating Nariman from his debts was the only thing on Chandra's mind. The doctors at Bombay Hospital delivered the bad news that Nariman's sugar was now out of control. The man was in a state of coma.

Dr Dholakia did what he could but it was beyond his control. When Nariman passed away on 10 December 1977, Chandra was by his side. What was meant to be a simple hip surgery was hampered by diabetes.

By his own admission, Chandra had learnt the most from

Nariman. The man was a father figure to the young director and the thought of him not being around was too much to bear. *Don* was started just for Nariman and the effort sadly seemed in vain. For the thirty-five-year-old director, the occasion seemed a little too overwhelming.

Determination took charge of the precarious situation and Chandra assured Nariman's family that their financial woes would be over in no time. They just had to wait for the film to be released. The job on hand was to take stock of the situation and decide on the next course of action. It was clear that everyone who was involved with *Don* would need to meet at the earliest and take the film to its logical conclusion. Over the next few days, Chandra quickly called Amitabh, Zeenat, Pran, Salim and Javed to decide when they could meet and update them on the film. It was agreed that they all would congregate in Salim's house (now the famous Galaxy Apartments) in Bandra in a week.

Chandra was determined on *Don* not being a jinxed film. There were just too many producers and directors whose films had remained incomplete after they had passed away or just because money was hard to come by. That thought was too much for Chandra to bear and he just hoped that the all-important meeting would transpire without any glitches. For now, it was time for a silent prayer for Nariman.

CHAPTER FIFTEEN

On a budget of ₹85 lakh, there was no way *Don* could be called an inexpensive film. Yes, *Sholay* was made at ₹3 crore but it was a multi-starrer and had the Sippy brand name which was a huge advantage. What Nariman and Chandra were intensely aware of at the time of announcing the film in July 1974 was that a large chunk of the film's finances would have to come from the distributors.

This was an era when the pre-sale of a film's key components like satellite rights and music were unheard of. There was some money to be made in music though it was apparent that the equation was hopelessly in favour of the music company. Only a big producer or an established director could make a difference when it came to negotiating with a music label. Neither Nariman nor Chandra could lay any claim to either title.

As things worked out, 60% of the film's budget came from the distributors. They were convinced by the increasing bankability of Amitabh as a star and Salim–Javed as a capable writing duo. The presence of Kalyanji–Anandji was a source of comfort as well. The worry was the remaining 40 per cent which the producer and the director hoped would come from somewhere as the film was being made. It was this kind of raw self-belief that ensured *Don* was filmed. Today, it could well be termed foolishness and, to many others, just plain stupidity.

The Hindi film industry then—and even today—is split into territories whose names are a serious hangover from the colonial rule. In all, there are fourteen territories, which include East Punjab, Nizam, Central India and Central Provinces Berar. Given that the success of a Hindi film depends greatly on states in the North and the West, these regions are where the distribution rights fetch the highest amount of money. In the case of *Don*, distributors in six territories agreed to acquire the rights to the film at ₹12 lakh each. These six were Delhi/Uttar Pradesh, Central Province, West Bengal, Bihar, Nizam/Andhra and Bombay, as it was still known then.

Much of this would come after the film was completed or as the film was being made, which meant that there had to be a continuous flow of cash throughout the making of the film. This was necessary to ensure that the shooting was never affected. It was apparent that very little could come from Nariman given the colossal failure of *Zindagi Zindagi*. Eventually, of the 40 per cent of the ₹85 lakh budget, which worked out to a little over ₹30 lakh, at least ₹7 lakh came from Chandra. This was not exactly loose change and the young director was quite aware of this. With the passing away of Nariman, much of this would have to be resolved or at least given some sense of clarity. At least that's what Chandra hoped as the meeting at Salim's house was drawing close.

It was an interesting mix of people at the writer's house. There was Ranjit Motwani, a prominent lawyer in the film industry, Chandra and Salim. Yash Johar, who had worked with Dev Anand in the production of box-office successes like *Guide*, *Jewel Thief*, *Prem Pujari* and *Hare Rama Hare Krishna*, was to play the good samaritan. He had just launched his banner by the name of Dharma Productions with the debut film *Dostana* starring Amitabh, Shatrughan and Zeenat and it was set to be released in about two years.

Salim suggested a straightforward method where the distribution rights for the film could be sold for a revised sum of ₹21 lakh instead of the original ₹12 lakh. His opinion was that *Don* had the ingredients of a box-office success and could command that price. What was left unsaid was that his own reputation as a part of a successful writing duo had soared. This was on the back of a new, established star whose stock was merely improving with each film. It was agreed that this increased amount of ₹9 lakh would be given to Nariman's wife, Salma, and their three children. The gesture was spontaneously seconded by all.

Meanwhile, the lucrative Bombay territory, which included the city and its suburbs, Gujarat and parts of Maharashtra and Karnataka, was acquired by Mavji Shah, who was Kalyanji–Anandji's brother. Mavji, who initially objected to the higher price, was later convinced by all that it was a safe bet. The deal was simple. He would hold the rights for suburbs and the city and sell the balance in parts. He figured this arrangement would fetch ₹21 lakh.

Now, the tricky part was the 40 per cent for which the source of funding had never been decided. If the film was to be completed, it was clear that some corners would have to be cut. Amitabh, who was scheduled to get ₹2.5 lakh for the film, said that he would let go of ₹1.5 lakh, while Zeenat said that she did not want her ₹1.5 lakh fee at all. Pran, who was to be paid ₹5 lakh, was fine with half that amount. What was left was the fee to be paid to the director.

Chandra's agreement with Nariman on a three bedroom flat in Bandra was now just a spoken word and nothing more. Of course, that was in the event of the film becoming a hit. The bigger worry was the ₹3.5 lakh that Chandra had rustled from friends and well-wishers. Over the last couple of years, the producer had managed to return ₹2 lakh. The issue was the balance, which Nariman was seriously embarrassed about. Eventually, it was agreed that Chandra would get ₹1 lakh as the director's fee. How the contours of that meeting might have changed if the success of *Don* was known to some soothsayer is today merely academic.

A quick status check of *Don* was also undertaken and there was exactly one scene left to be filmed. It was the one where Amitabh would break into Shetty's house as the latter settles into his evening drink. It is at this point where Shetty reveals Om's real identity and the secret behind Iftekhar's murder is revealed to the audience. Amitabh yelling 'Shakaal' repeatedly at the end of the scene has remained in the audience's mind. About two and a half years later, Ramesh Sippy's *Shaan* would have Kulbhushan Kharbanda playing the villain with Shakaal as his screen name.

By Chandra's own estimate, the scene between Amitabh and Shetty required two days of shooting. Help came from Sultan Ahmed, who was on the verge of wrapping up work on *Ganga Ki Saugandh*, a film that he was producing and directing. This starred Amitabh, Rekha and Amjad Khan. Sultan loaned his Bandra apartment to Chandra for this all-important sequence in *Don*. Once the shot was in the bag, Chandra started to think of post-production. The possibility of shooting an additional song was not even on the most distant horizon. Not only would it be shot but it would be one that *Don* would come to be remembered for.

CHAPTER SIXTEEN

Bandra, Mumbai's upmarket suburb, has an extremely close connection with films. If Mehboob Studios is one landmark, others include 'Aashirwaad', Rajesh Khanna's sea-facing bungalow on Carter Road, Hrishikesh Mukherjee's house and Shah Rukh Khan's 'Mannat'. Of course, a lot of other well-known names in Bollywood like Subhash Ghai and Sanjay Dutt have been living there for many years. The most well-known resident in Bandra remains Dilip Kumar whose bungalow has, for years, been the venue for tinsel town's famous parties. Anyone from Mumbai's film industry still swears by the thespian's hospitality, which includes the best fare in town.

Chandra's deep friendship with Dilip resulted in innumerable visits to the bungalow. On one such visit which, not surprisingly, stretched through the day, he was intently taking a look at a script called 'Master', based on *My Fair Lady*, that Dilip had written. Ever since *Don* was almost done, Chandra had been pondering his next move and had almost decided to start work on a film based on Dilip's script. Just then, Javed Akhtar and Ramesh Sippy, who was still reeling under the success of *Sholay*, walked in. Dilip, Chandra and the two gentlemen began a relaxed conversation. A lot of people had already watched the trials of *Don* and Ramesh, like many others, had quite liked the film. Lunch was served and a few minutes later, they were joined by Manoj who was visibly busy with his work.

Manoj was just starting work on *Kranti* and was keen on discussing the project with Dilip. By the time it was released in early 1981, *Kranti* would be Dilip's first film in five years. Chandra greeted Manoj warmly and Dilip was quick to seize the opportunity. 'Kamaal hai. So many big directors are in my house today,' he said. Manoj was visibly embarrassed and Dilip quickly asked him if he had seen *Don.* Manoj replied in the negative and Chandra did not miss the expression on his mentor's face.

When they had a moment of privacy, a slightly livid Manoj came straight to the point. 'Yaar Chandra, hundreds of people have seen the film. How come you did not show it to me?' he asked. The young director was profusely apologetic and quickly organized a private screening for Manoj and Javed, who too was keen on seeing the final product.

The following day, Chandra, seated beside Manoj, proudly showed his film. The film progressed smoothly and Manoj was engrossed. Always a man of few words, Manoj started fidgeting about half hour before the film was done. Once it was through, he warmly congratulated Chandra and decided to speak his mind. 'Very good film. The only problem is that the second half is just too packed. You need to have a song before the climax to reduce the tension. There is not even time to go to the loo after a drink during the interval,' he said. Chandra was stunned and knew he had his task cut out. Where could he possibly get a song from at this point?

To this day, Manoj laughs heartily about that incident. Lighting a cigarette, he says he actually recommended two songs. 'My feeling was that the film was heavy and needed some relief. When the audience pays for tickets, it is to watch entertainment,' is his view. The last thing you want is the audience asking you a question like 'Where is the entertainment?'

Besides, Manoj, no novice to understanding how music can make or break a film, believes that every scene in a film has a raaga in it. 'That is how good music is created. When I sit with the music director, my ear is my heart and I fully understand that people love melody,' he says with that familiar twinkle in his eye.

Realizing that there could be a potential crisis, Chandra approached Kalyanji–Anandji, who were calm and asked him to come over to the studio. The young man, who was barely breathing, told them what Manoj had thought of the film. The duo asked him to relax and they agreed to meet again in a day or two. Chandra was still receiving feedback on *Don*. While he graciously thanked everyone for what they said, it was a chance remark by a lady that caught his attention. Reema, Raj Kapoor's daughter, had heard a lot about the film from Zeenat and requested Chandra to send the tins of prints. When he told her it was a rush print and required dubbing, she said, 'I am Raj Kapoor's daughter, I know what a rush print is!' Once Reema saw the print that Chandra sent to R.K. Studios, she called the director and said, 'Very entertaining, Chandra. I am very angry you killed the street singer. You must bring back the lungiwallah Amitabh later in the film,' as she gently replaced the phone receiver. 'Can we have a song around the lungiwallah?' was the thought that kept Chandra occupied.

The only hitch was that the hero was very well-dressed in

the second half. Chandra decided to have a song when the hero, who is on the run, meets the group from Uttar Pradesh. The timing for the song was perfect and made him happy, but he was still worried about the song.

At dawn, he rushed to Kalyanji–Anandji and explained what he had in mind. They agreed with Chandra and told him that they had a slow song that they were still working on. It had a Bhojpuri feel to it and the feeling was that it could work in *Don*. The pace had to be worked on and the music duo promised to work on that. The meeting was also attended by Javed and Anjaan, the lyricist. In the latter's view, recent songs of his that had words like Ganga and Banaras were doing very well. Given Amitabh's own Allahabad background, everything fell in place. It was funny how Manoj had a small hand to play in both 'Yeh Mera Dil' and this song at the last minute.

The extent to which Kalyanji–Anandji made an impact on the Hindi film industry is not really very well known nor has it been documented with any level of skill. Their music hall on Peddar Road had the likes of Rajesh, Jeetendra and Shashi drop by casually and spend hours chatting about everything including films. Anandji recalls that phase very fondly and says it was great growing up in Girgaum, an area in south Mumbai, with people like Rajesh and Jeetendra for neighbours. 'It had a great atmosphere and there was a lot of filmi influence. As a young man, I remember going to the Strand cinema to watch *A Patch of Blue*.' Their interest in films and music were given a strong foundation here.

Ila Arun, who would many years later make her name as a folk-song specialist with numbers like *Choli Ke Peeche*, worked very closely with the duo. Laxmikant–Pyarelal, a name that would come to be associated with films like *Dosti*, *Do Raaste*, *Bobby*, *Daag*, *Amar Akbar Anthony*, *Sargam* and *Karz*, were assistants to Kalyanji–Anandji for a decade till 1963. Sapna Mukherjee would be launched by the duo in *Jaanbaaz* in 1986. In the 1970s, the Kalyanji–Anandji school of music was among the most successful that the Hindi film industry had seen. The interesting part is that the Western influence was starting to show in their music. 'I think it was quite obvious in *Purab Aur Paschim* itself,' thinks Anandji.

Funnily enough, when the script for *Don* was first narrated to Kalyanji–Anandji, they had looked at each other a little quizzically. They had the same thought in their minds. There was no scope for music in a story like this. 'At that point, Nariman and Chandra drew a caricature to describe the character. It was that of a boy running and my brother and I

Chandra, Kanchan and Anandji at the recording of the music for *Don* at Film Centre in Tardeo

were quite amused to see that,' he says, barely managing to control his laughter.

More importantly, it convinced the music duo that a different kind of music could be created for this racy film. Ananji maintains that this period was important in terms of a transition in Hindi films. 'Scripts were getting tighter and music had to change with the changing times. All this meant that musicians had to look for newer ideas and be more creative,' he says. If *Purab Aur Paschim*, as he puts it, was really about fusion music, the duo decided to use instruments like rototoms and synthesizers for *Don*. There was one other thing they were determined on. 'We decided to give the best background that we could for the film. Instinctively, we knew the film needed that,' says Anandji. His favourite background is in the scene where Don is chased by the police and tries getting on to the train.

The need to integrate a song with the script was impressed upon them by Manoj, though Anandji says it was inculcated early in the day by I.S. Johar. Kalyanji–Anandji composed the music for Johar in films like *Johar-Mehmood in Goa* and *Johar in Kashmir*. 'Normally, Kalyanji and I would compose two tunes and play both to the director,' he says.

'Music has to occur to me. It was just luck that gave me that one line,' is Anandji's view. It is that frenetic pace of work that the duo used and each of the songs in *Don* was composed in less than half an hour. There was no thought of creating a masterpiece or an evergreen song. They just wanted to compose good music.

Complementing them were Anjaan and Indivar, two of the finest lyricists. Anjaan, for years, had given handwritten lyrics to Kalyanji–Anandji and was instrumental in writing songs like 'Hum Hain Banarasi Babu' and 'Ganga Maiya Mein

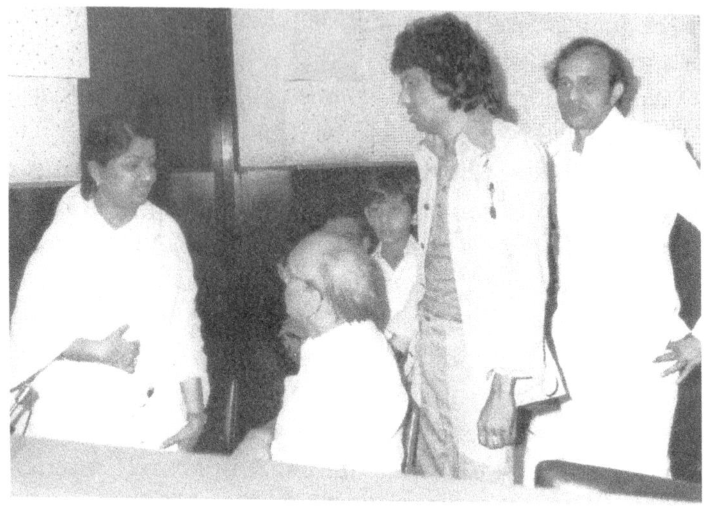

Lata Mangeshkar, Chandra and Kalyanji with sound recordist Kaushik at the recording of 'Jiska Mujhe Tha Intezaar'

Jab Tak Pani Rahe'. Indivar was the romantic specialist and was behind songs like 'Chandan Sa Badan'. Another lyricist who came from the Kalyanji–Anandji camp was Gulshan Bawra who would write memorable songs like 'Mere Desh Ki Dharti', 'Yaari Hai Imaan Mera' and 'Kasme Vaade Nibhayenge Hum'. Often, people wondered what Kalyanji and Anandji were like individually. If Kalyanji had a classical bent of mind, Anandji was the creative maverick who found his rhythm singing in the bathroom. It is something that Anandji easily acknowledges. 'Kalyanji was the poet. I am still the sort who gets the idea on the spur of the moment and then works on it,' he says very subtly. In the case of *Don,* it was pretty much Anandji all the way.

For Chandra, it was a weird feeling to be surrounded by stars of this magnitude. A novice director was with veterans

Chandra with Indivar at the recording of the music for *Don*

who knew their craft remarkably well. It certainly was not bad company to keep.

When Chandra got in touch with HMV (then known as the Gramophone Company of India Limited with the iconic dog logo), he initially went with three songs and the title music of *Don*. This was the time when the company had just moved from the 78 rpm format to 45 rpm, with the latter being the size of a CD. Audio cassettes were still a few years away and music was in a different phase then.

Vijay Kishore Dubey, who was then the head of A&R at HMV, was the decision maker. Known as Dubey *saab* to the people who worked with him, he had spent time working in Radio Ceylon before moving to HMV's office on PM Road in Mumbai in the mid-1960s. Dubey was a chain smoker and of medium height. Those who have worked with him remember him as a talkative, enthusiastic man who was always bubbling with ideas. Wearing a trademark silk bush shirt, Dubey was credited with exporting HMV's repertoire to destinations like Sri Lanka, Singapore and Malaysia. His biggest contributions were compilations like *Hits of Kishore* or *Duets of Kishore and Lata.*

When Dubey met Chandra, he was forthright. He needed twenty-two minutes of music and the material that Chandra had provided was woefully inadequate. The young director was livid, to say the least, and said that he had to be taken a lot more seriously. This was after Chandra saw a huge 12" double folder in colour for Nasir Hussain's *Zamaane Ko Dikhana Hai.* By contrast, *Don* got something made of thin paper. After a bit of a showdown, he walked out. Chandra

Chandra, Manhar Udhas, Kishore, Anjaan and Kalyanji recording the music for *Don*

had absolutely no inkling of what was to follow and, when he met Dubey a few days later, he was embarrassed to find the music of *Don* in a double folder with Chandra's face at the back of the record. Dubey was politely told that the star of the film was Amitabh and some laughter saved the day. It is rumoured that some enthusiastic collectors are still in possession of the record with Chandra's picture. That would be worth a fortune today.

In those times, any director like Chandra would get lyricists to write three stanzas for any song. Eventually, just two would be picturised. The reason for this was simple. It was commonly believed that the audience's patience would drop after two stanzas. The longer version of the song would be saved for the record. In the case of 'Main Hoon Don', it had a running time of 3 minutes 28 seconds on screen, while the one on the record was four minutes forty-three seconds. To get to a total running time of twenty-two minutes, the additional stanza was required. Chandra was still falling short and 'Khaike Paan Banaraswala' would come to his rescue. And that too in style.

When Kalyanji–Anandji played the new composition to Chandra, he was delighted. It had a nice beat and would require Amitabh to dance. The director knew he could convince his hero and did not allow that to bother him. Since Kishore Kumar had been Amitabh's voice for *Don* and for many films prior to it as well, there was no question of looking elsewhere. It was time to record the song and get it into the film.

In a couple of days, Chandra, Kalyanji–Anandji and their entourage were at Film Centre in Tardeo, a well-known haunt for everyone in the industry. At the appointed hour, Kishore turned up and looked positively bright. He was attired in a checked lungi and was mysteriously carrying a bag. Meanwhile, Nariman and Chandra had arranged for a screening of 'Yeh Hai Bambai Nagaria' for Kishore to see. 'Dada, you have to outdo this number,' was all Nariman said. He asked for a large plastic packet and said he would be ready to record in a few minutes. Quickly, he fished out a large packet with about a dozen paans. He popped one after the other into his mouth and just continued spitting. There was a look of bewilderment on Chandra's face till he was gently told by Kalyanji–Anandji that the song would turn out like a dream. Anandji remembers the recording of the song with great fondness. 'Anjaan, Babla, Javed and I created a great atmosphere and Kishore Kumar gave us a great song,' he says.

Kishore dressed in a lungi at the recording of 'Khaike Paan'. With him are Babla and Anjaan (courtesy Babla)

As Kishore began singing, Chandra realized what the man was made of. There was no question he was sounding like Amitabh. This was the master of modulation at work and Chandra himself heard how this man could sound like Amitabh, Rajesh, Sanjeev or Dev. In fact, there was no facet to music that the man did not know. Being a genius and an eccentric at the same time came easily to Kishore and that day, he was just being himself.

The song brings back some great memories for Babla as well. 'Khaike was a big hit in the West Indies and we had a calypso version as well. My wife Kanchan and I were always asked for this song when we travelled there and it was a smash hit,' he says very fondly. In the film's titles, Babla's name appears as music assistant, though his involvement was unquestionable at every stage of its music composition. Often called the rhythm king, Babla recalls the experience of performing live shows in the 1970s and thereafter. 'Music from Bollywood began to go international. It was the time when people came out and paid money to watch our actors perform and listen to our music,' he says.

Today, Babla says the Western feel to the theme in *Don* was what drew him to the project. 'It was the foundation on which I would compose my music in the later years,' he thinks as he proudly shows pictures of his wife, Kanchan, and him performing at several venues across the world. 'I still find it funny when people say we created the early audience for live shows in countries like the US, UK and the West Indies. In those days, we only worked for joy and never thought of money,' he says with a broad smile. Babla and Kanchan formed a very successful musical duo and their live shows were a big draw.

When Chandra first heard the song, his mind was drifting

to how he would picturize it. He called Amitabh and Zeenat and briefed them on the song. Once that was done, he got the crew together over the next few days. This was far more complicated than what Chandra had anticipated. After all, this song was a last minute addition and it had to fit into the story without a hitch.

Amitabh least expected to dance again in the film. To his credit, he was remarkably elegant for a man so tall. Luckily, he also possessed a great sense of rhythm and, throughout the filming of *Don*, Chandra found it hard to recollect too many instances when the artist did not get it right the first time. In fact, the five songs in the film were all filmed in less than two weeks.

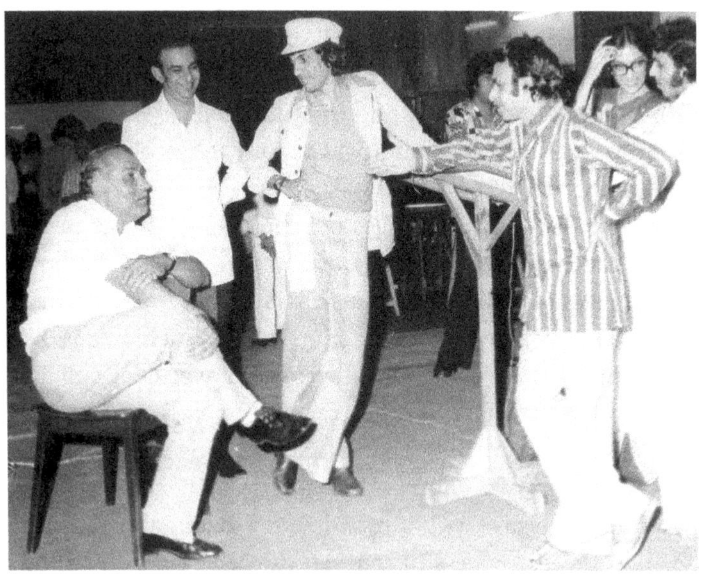

Nariman, Mavji Shah, Chandra and Anandji recording the music for *Don*. Also seen are Babla and Nutan

Chandra, Indivar and Kalyanji during the music recording for *Don*

This time, the star decided to spend some time listening to the song. P.L. Raj too took time out to think a little harder. While it was similar to 'Yeh Hai Bambai Nagaria', the situation was slightly different since Amitabh was not dressed in a lungi. A few days later, Amitabh came to Chandra with a broad smile. 'Chandra, Abhishek dances very funnily when I play this song. He hops with one leg and drifts out of the frame. I quite like that step of his,' he said. The director was quite amused and did not quite expect a toddler to be the star of the moment. When Chandra shouted roll he did not forget to say, 'A step dedicated to Junior Amitabh Bachchan.' To this day, Amitabh maintains that it was the step where he moves sideways and is a lift from what Abhishek did. To most people, the song also highlighted the influence of Bhagwan

Dada and, in a few years, Amitabh's dance steps would be the beginning of a trend.

To give the song a more authentic look and feel, the hero did something quite similar to what Kishore had done. He chewed one paan after the other till his lips were looking so stained that Chandra had little option but to say 'Action!'

The worry was that Zeenat was not having it easy when it came to finding her groove in the song. This was the real UP-song and the lady was not really comfortable. Chandra calmly told her to think of the shooting venue as a discotheque. 'Just go for it and give that normal disco step. Leave the rest to me,' was all he said. With that confidence, Zeenat just eased into the song and it was soon over. Moolchand, the man with the pot belly, was another attraction in the number and there are more than a handful of viewers who still love watching him.

At the end of the filming of the song, Raj and Chandra warmly congratulated each other. Actually, Chandra was still preoccupied with the fate of his film's music. He wondered what Dubey's verdict would be. Less than a week later, he would call to say that HMV would be delighted to buy the music of *Don*.

To Chandra, the objective from the first day of shooting was to make a thriller. The Bond hangover was too much and he wanted a slick product that kept the audience at the edge of their seats. In that sense, every song needed a clear reason and justification to be there. He always referred to songs as hand brakes.

If he was convinced about the first four he had filmed, 'Khaike Paan' was the one he was not completely sure about.

An Amul advertisement that took off on the huge success of 'Khaike Paan'.
(Courtesy: Amul and daCunha Communications)

Great song though it was, the extent to which it seamlessly integrated was a bit of a debate in his own mind. To this day, he holds a slight belief (and only a slight) that 'Khaike Paan' was a bit of a compromise, though he is the first to admit that the viewers loved it.

Even Kishore was a bit taken aback by the success of the song. The music of the film was in the market by then and the singer was busy recording other songs, in addition to performing live shows. In one show in Madras, as the city was known then, the audience was really coming to life. Kishore was joined by Amitabh on this visit. Quite suddenly, someone in the audience asked for the paan song. A slightly lost Kishore was wondering which song it was till Amitabh reminded him it was the one from *Don.* Sportingly, Kishore agreed and the audience was thrilled.

Once he was back in Mumbai, the first person Kishore called was Anandji. 'This song is going to be a huge hit. I had a request to sing it from Madras of all places,' he said. The conversation did not end there. Kishore told the musician that the next time he sang this song at a live show he would charge another ₹5,000. Knowing the singer's great sense of humour, Anandji thought he was joking.

Far from it, as he was to discover. Unfailingly, Kishore would be asked for the song at each show and he would quickly come for his money at the end of it. 'I decided this game had to come to an end,' says Anandji with a loud laugh. He did not have to wait too long.

Just a few days later, there was a live concert in the city's Shanmukhananda Hall. Anandji noticed a young boy who was enthusiastically humming each song with Kishore. He winked at the boy and asked him to come backstage for a moment. The lad obliged as the musician whispered something into his ears and the two then shook hands.

Shortly, the young boy ran on to the stage and touched Kishore's feet and said there was no singer like him ever. A visibly embarrassed Kishore hugged him warmly and the boy then said he wanted to sing a song. The singer was game and the audience was quite enjoying the occasion. Grabbing the mike, the boy's first lines were 'O Chhora Ganga Kinare Wala' from 'Khaike Paan Banaraswala'. Kishore then had no option but to sing the song from the middle without the

'Arrey Bhang Ka Rang Jama Ho Chakachak' introduction. After the show, he came to Anandji and complimented him on his ingenuity. That was the last time Kishore ever made a request for ₹5,000 for singing 'Khaike Paan'.

There was never a live concert without this song. Invariably, the first song was 'Main Hoon Don' and the finale was 'Khaike Paan Banaraswala'. People who have sat through any concert can hardly remember a foot that was not tapping when Kishore belted out these two songs.

The best example of the audience's approval was to take place in the 1978 Ganpati celebration in the city's thickly populated Lalbaug area. The moment the two songs were played, the crowd went ballistic. Chandra was taken aback by what he saw and, understandably, pleased as well. When the crowd asked for a repeat of both the songs, he could not hold himself back any more. He found a place where he could get some privacy and looked back at the crowd and the large Ganpati idol. Suddenly, he felt overwhelmed by the whole occasion and thought of the man who was not with him any more. At that very moment, Chandra broke down. He felt extremely lost in that large crowd.

CHAPTER SEVENTEEN

The comment by Devyani Chaubal in *Star & Style* magazine was the worst possible start to Chandra's morning. It had been a little over a week since *Don* was released and the gossip in the film trade was already giving the director some sleepless nights. The only consolation was that the second week's collections were an improvement from the disastrous first.

Released on 12 May, *Don* had a very low profile entry into theatres compared to most other films in 1978. 'The career of a young man is over,' was what Devyani (Devi to most people in the industry) said. It was a terse remark and irked Chandra like nothing had in several years. He had sweated it out for four years to ensure this project saw the light of day and this journalist had quite ruthlessly written off the film.

It was not as if *Don* was going to have it easy. Exactly a week before it was released, Yash Chopra's multi-starrer *Trishul* had already hit theatres across India. With a line up that included names like Amitabh, Sanjeev and Shashi, what chance did Chandra have as a debutante? Very little by his own admission, though it was just his bad luck that 1978 was one of those years when some of the biggest directors would make their presence felt. Apart from Yash, there was Prakash Mehra's *Muqaddar Ka Sikandar,* Raj Kapoor's *Satyam Shivam Sundaram* and Satyajit Ray's *Shatranj Ke Khilari.* Raj Khosla's *Main Tulsi Tere Aangan Ki* too was another big one. Amitabh was in the thick of it that year with more releases like *Besharam, Ganga Ki Saugandh* and *Kasme Vaade.*

For Yash, the good news continued. *Trishul* was just an extension of his dream run with Amitabh after *Deewar* and *Kabhi Kabhie.* People were kicked after watching his latest film, which had great performances by all coupled with some pretty good music. Salim–Javed had given the director a good script and the plot was aided by some vintage one-liners.

Deep down, Chandra remained quietly confident about *Don.* He wrapped up his breakfast and was quickly on the phone tracking the prospects of his film. Without exception, everyone who had watched *Don* liked it and it was odd that Devi had written what she did. With a limited budget for publicity, Chandra was not in a position to promote his film as well as the other directors. The other big advantage was that they had the help of financially sound producers like Gulshan Rai, who could get the best theatres for the films. No such luck for this young man who was left to do everything on his own. He also wondered if showing the first couple of scenes of *Don* to Deven Verma was a mistake. Anyway, it was too late to regret any decision.

Don was released with one hundred and twenty prints and Chandra had a tough time with the theatre owners who seemed far more inclined to go with *Trishul.* The first week was the most difficult and it was then that the news on 'Khaike Paan' creating an effect on the audience came in. Probably Devi had jumped the gun, thought Chandra to himself.

A crowd outside New Excelsior theatre in Mumbai for the advance booking of *Don*

On an impulse, he decided to visit New Excelsior, a well-known theatre in south Mumbai. He walked past unrecognized and saw the full impact of *Don* on his audience. The first shot on the screen was a picture of Nariman to whom the film was dedicated. It was a difficult moment and Chandra managed to hold himself together. Listening to the buzz in the hall, it was apparent that the audience was intrigued about seeing Amitabh as a villain and remained convinced that the hero—the good one in their mind—would appear sooner than later. The constant buzz in the hall reached a high when Helen gyrated to 'Yeh Mera Dil' and the tapping of feet amused him.

Yes, the first half was captivating and that was the key. To Chandra, the source of comfort was that the audience was not set to go home and was instead keen to know how the story would play out. When Kishore belted out 'Khaike Paan', the transformation in the hall had to be seen to be believed. The audience was on its feet and the dancing was impromptu. Through the length of the song, Chandra could barely hear a word of the song on the screen. The din in the theatre was something he had seldom encountered. He just grinned sheepishly and thought fondly of Manoj. At the end of that show, the first person Chandra placed a call to was Manoj and he just played out the reaction from his audience with a childlike delight. The mentor was calm and said he knew the film would click.

The thought of Deven crossed Chandra's mind again. When *Don* was ready for dubbing, Chandra decided to go for the facility at B.R. Studios, where there was an important technological breakthrough. For the first time, it was now possible for an artist to listen to his or her voice after the dubbing was done. The big advantage was that there was a lot of room for improvement at a very minimal cost.

Chandra was excited about this and *Don* was the first film to be dubbed at B.R. Sound & Music, the dubbing and music division of the studio. He was scheduled to work with G.S. Bhatia, who would, in time, be involved in films like *The Burning Train*, *Insaaf Ka Tarazu*, *Disco Dancer* and *Saaransh*.

It was time to record the first scene when Amitabh makes his entry in the car to face the three men. As luck would have it, the man with the beard (Raj Singh in the film) did not turn up. A slightly edgy Chandra spotted Deven who was at the studio waiting to dub for his forthcoming directorial release, *Besharam*. Both men quickly chatted up and Chandra asked Deven if he could lend his voice to Raj Singh. Deven immediately agreed and the job was done in a few minutes. As he was leaving, he asked Chandra if he could see the first scenes of *Don*. The young director agreed and for the next couple of minutes, Deven was quiet and almost transfixed. At the end of it, he wished Chandra the very best and said he really liked what he saw.

Besharam was released in March 1978 and the feedback on the film was not very good. One of Chandra's assistants rushed to him to say that the titles in the film with the psychedelic array of colours looked remarkably similar to *Don*. It took several minutes for Chandra to understand what had been conveyed and he calmly said, 'Imitation is the best form of flattery.' Eventually, *Besharam* was not a commercial success and this fact has not been noticed at all.

A slightly tacky bunch of papers held Sunil's attention as he was waiting to go to school. The twelve-year old was near Kurla station and saw *Don ke Poorna Samwad* written on the first sheet of a roadside stall. He quickly spoke to the stall owner who said it would cost char anna (25 paise). Amitabh Bachchan already held the fancy of the lad and the money he had kept aside for a little drink at the end of school was worth a miss.

The bunch of papers had the complete dialogues of *Don* written in crude ink that promised to smudge Sunil's white shirt. Over the next week, the lad had memorized every line from that bunch and was ready to watch the film. These were the dialogues in a pirated form for the avid viewer at a princely price.

Over the next two days, Sunil and his neighbours in Kalina's Air India Colony sat with the newspapers and decided to catch the 3 p.m. show at Roopam Cinema in Sion. That was a bit of a bus ride from where the boys lived and Sunil wondered why *Don* was not playing in any of the screens close to where he lived. Years later, he would realize that all the well-known theatres like Sheetal, Akash and Bharat where he had watched *Zanjeer* and *Sholay* were not comfortable showing an unknown film called *Don*.

Tickets then were not cheap and came as a reward for doing well in the term examinations. Sunil had to really study hard this time around if he had to watch both *Trishul* and *Don*. He did exactly that and some money quickly came his way. At ₹4.50 for a balcony ticket, the young kids were mouthing Amitabh's dialogues with him. In some cases, they said it before their hero.

Most people who watched *Don* did so after *Trishul*. If the latter was about Amitabh playing a Delhi-based businessman, *Don* was very mass-oriented, action-packed and certainly very in-your-face. The music too was cool and there was a chance to watch the hero in a double role. It was really a treat and the audience came in droves.

In those days, when the success of a film depended so greatly on its music, *Don* was helped a great deal by repeated requests from radio listeners who did not seem to get enough of its songs. In 1978, Ameen Sayani's *Binaca Geetmala* repeatedly played 'Yeh Mera Dil', 'Khaike Paan' and 'Main Hoon Don'. Other songs from films like *Ghar*, *Shalimar*, *Des Pardes*, *Trishul* and *Muqaddar Ka Sikandar* too made their mark. But, all said and done, when 'Khaike Paan' was played, nothing really could come close to it.

Without a doubt, Chandra did not anticipate *Don* to take off the way it did. It ran for an unbelievable fifty weeks in most centres in India while it did seventy-five weeks in Hyderabad.

Hari Pamnani, to this day, remains stunned by the success of the film. After all, his family acquired the distribution rights for *Don* for the Nizam territory. This covered the city of Hyderabad and the rest of Andhra Pradesh and parts of Maharashtra like Aurangabad. On an investment of ₹3 lakhs, his family raked in revenues of ₹15 lakh.

Hari, who is today in his mid-60s, remembers the film picking up very slowly. 'We were not too confident and, actually, a little worried as well,' he says. Eventually, it was at the Tarakarama theatre, a property owned by N.T. Rama Rao, where *Don* set this record. There were four shows starting at 12 noon all the way to 9 p.m. and the crowds just did not stop. This was not the first film that Pamnani or his family was distributing. In 1974, they released the Vinod Khanna

Chandra in Hyderabad receiving the award for *Don*'s platinum jubilee — end 1979

and Tanuja starrer, *Imtihaan*, and, in the following year, it was *Umar Qaid* that had Sunil Dutt, Jeetendra and Vinod Mehra.

The family released their films through a distribution company called Bombay Films. 'In fact, our first project was an English film, *Eyewitness*, which was released in 1970,' says Hari. His family owned Bombay Halwa House, a well-known sweet shop in Hyderabad and the film connection was really unplanned. 'We got to know Nariman through some of our contacts and that is how we got pulled into *Don*,' recalls Hari.

For the Nizam circuit, they purchased just six prints initially and it turned out to be their best investment. 'Amitabh came to Hyderabad when the film had completed its silver jubilee and things just came to a standstill. He was God to his large audience by that time,' laughs Hari as he narrates the story.

Chandra would fly to Hyderabad a year later to pick up the award for the platinum jubilee of *Don*. There was more than one reason to feel happy. After all, this was not the first award that the film was going to win. He was clearly on a roll.

CHAPTER EIGHTEEN

It was a moment of uncontrollable joy for Saira Banu as she rushed into Chandra's home with her mother, Naseem Banu, in early 1979. The news was not just good but completely unexpected as well. '*Don* has won three Filmfare awards,' was all that the lady said. She had brought a large bouquet which she affectionately gave the stunned director. The results of the much sought-after awards had just been announced. For a film that had a disastrous opening and was considered to be an inedible concoction between a flop producer and an inexperienced director, this was an overwhelming moment.

Chandra just sank into the large sofa of his living room and allowed himself a while before the enormity of the news made any sense to him. The award for the Best Actor had come to Amitabh for the second year in a row after he had won it for *Amar Akbar Anthony* in 1978. In 1979, *Don* was nominated in five categories and eventually won it in three.

It scarcely mattered to Chandra that he had not won the award for the Best Director. In fact, he was not even nominated and that prized list had names like Satyajit Ray, Prakash Mehra, Yash Chopra, Raj Kapoor and Raj Khosla.

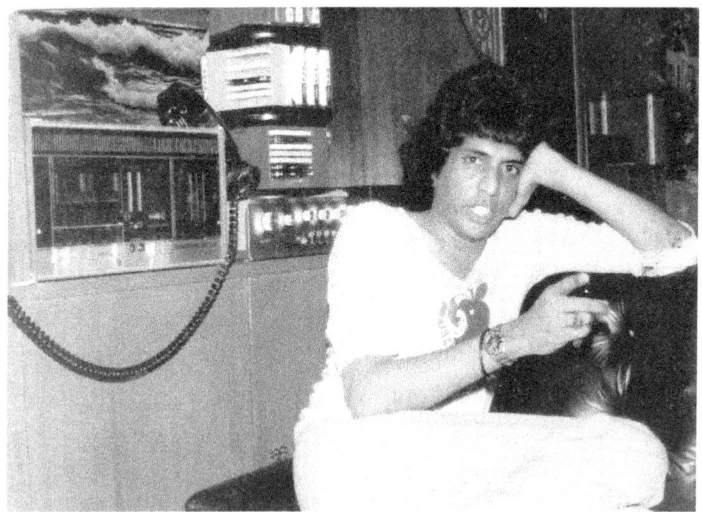

Chandra at home in mid-1979 relishing the success of *Don*

Given that this had the names of seasoned directors, Chandra himself knew that it would be too much for a debutante to make the cut. The final winner was Satyajit Ray for *Shatranj Ke Khilari*.

It was incredible that Amitabh was nominated for the Best Actor award for three films—*Don*, *Trishul* and *Muqaddar Ka Sikandar*. To win it for *Don* was confirmation that the actor's double role was well appreciated. Sanjeev was nominated for *Devata* and *Pati Patni Aur Woh*. Three years ago, when the two actors were again competing for the top honours, Sanjeev had won it for *Aandhi* while Amitabh had lost out in spite of a remarkable performance in *Deewar*.

The icing on the cake was that the best playback for both male and female went to *Don*. Kishore won it for 'Khaike Paan' and Asha for 'Yeh Mera Dil'. Kalyanji–Anandji were nominated in the Best Music category but the winners were Laxmikant-Pyarelal for *Satyam Shivam Sundaram*.

The huge acceptance of 'Khaike Paan' saw Anjaan being nominated for the Best Lyrics, which was finally won by Anand Bakshi for 'Aadmi Musafir Hai' in *Apnapan*. For *Don* to win three awards after nominations in five was more than what Chandra could have ever imagined. When his hero went on stage later that year in Mumbai's Shanmukhananda Hall, it was to a thunderous applause. When Amitabh posed for photographers with Nutan, who won the Best Actress award for *Main Tulsi Teri Aangan Ki*, it made for a very pretty picture indeed. The 26th Filmfare Awards of 1979 were, in more ways than one, an evening dominated by *Don*.

To this day, Chandra remains amused and somewhat perplexed when *Don* is referred to as a cult film. As much as no filmmaker sets out to make a blockbuster, it is impossible to make a cult film. It is probably fair to say that *Don* succeeded in influencing a certain generation of film lovers and certainly the ones beyond that as well. It denoted style, finesse, slickness and a cool attitude which is not remarkably different from what one sees in the Western films. Perhaps that's what made *Don* such an interesting topic for directors across India.

Interestingly, shades of *Don* are markedly visible in Shakti Samanta's *China Town* released in 1962. The concept of an undercover agent looking like a gangster was the theme there. The scene where the sole of the shoe is rotated is used to great effect in *China Town*. It is also the first scene in *Don* after the titles where Amitabh kills the gang member who is, in reality, a police informer.

The success of *China Town* at the box-office prompted remakes in Tamil as *Kudiyiruntha Kovil* with M.G.

Ramachandran and *Bhale Tammudu* in Telugu which had N.T. Rama Rao. Likewise, the phenomenal success of *Don* saw remakes again from the South. Rajinikanth was the hero in *Billa,* a 1980 smash hit. This had Helen again performing the same role that she had in *Don.* In the titles her name is mentioned as Helen (Bombay).

A year earlier, N.T. Rama Rao was again the hero in *Yugandhar,* the Telugu remake of *Don.* In both instances, 'Khaike Paan' was filmed with the local touch. Clearly, the success of the song in the original did not miss the attention of the directors. In Malayalam, the remake was *Shobaraj,* a 1986 release which had Mohanlal in the lead role.

Javed Akhtar's son Farhan, a self-confessed fan of *Don,* released his own version of the film *Don: The Chase Begins Again* in 2006 with Shah Rukh Khan in the lead role. The film was not only critically acclaimed but became one of the biggest hits of the year. The success prompted him to make a sequel to the remake, *Don 2: The Chase Continues,* which released in 2011. Not surprisingly, Farhan's projects saw remakes in Tamil and Telugu.

Don was not the first Amitabh film where he had played a double role. The audience had seen him doing that on screen in *Adalat* in 1976 and later in *Kasme Vaade* that hit the theatres less than a month before *Don.* Of course, the one in *Don* was what would be the most memorable for many years to come. Following *Don,* Amitabh would essay the double role in many a film like *The Great Gambler, Satte Pe Satta, Desh Premee, Aakhree Raasta* and even a triple role in *Mahaan.*

In time, every part of *Don* would become a fashion statement that made it a cult film. Be it Amitabh's sunglasses, his gait, the film's innumerable one-liners (fans still swear by lines like '*Don Zakhmi Hai To Kya Hua, Phir Bhi Don Hai*'), the theme music penned by Kalyanji–Anandji, Zeenat's boycut that became a rage or the 'Khaike Paan' number, the film ranks very high among its multitude of fans. In 2005, the beginning of 'Yeh Mera Dil' was used by The Black Eyed Peas, an American alternative hip-hop group, in their song, 'Don't Phunk with My Heart'. Later in the song, the melody and beats from 'Ae Naujawan Hai Sab Kuchh Yahan' song from *Apradh* were also used. In their capacity as original composers of both the songs, Kalyanji–Anandji were honoured with the BMI Award (Broadcast Music, Inc.) in 2006.

Of course, Chandra's stock also increased with the success of *Don*. His arrival as a filmmaker of some repute was confirmed when he was at Amitabh's Holi party in 1979. *Don* was a declared smash hit and Amitabh's mother called him and said, '*Beta, tumhari biradiri aa rahi hai.* People from your fraternity are coming. Please come.' He was touched and felt small in the company of Prakash Mehra, Manmohan Desai and Yash Chopra. Not bad at all for a director whose debut film was jinxed at several stages and could well have been shelved at almost any point of its making. Chandra was only well aware of what might not have been. For now, he was just lost in the revelry.

CHAPTER NINETEEN

Over three decades have passed since *Don* hit the theatres and the mystique around the film is still present. It has been ranked among Amitabh's finest performances and is a big draw on the home video circuit. Fans have confessed to watching it each time it is shown on satellite television and are often mouthing Salim–Javed's immortal one-liners with the hero. To its legion of fans and the multitude of folks who sell its DVD, it is simply called the *Original Don*.

Amitabh was already the big boss of the Hindi film industry and his dream run in 1978 merely confirmed that he was well and truly numero uno. In fact, most people think that he was pretty much No 1 to No 10 at his absolute peak. His films in the following years would confirm his titan-like status and if there was a bit of a question mark on their quality, it hardly mattered. The presence of the hero with that baritone was enough to fill the seats. That said, the impact of *Don* from the metamorphosis of the stylish villain into an equally impressive hero is hard to ignore.

Everyone in the star cast of *Don* only got bigger with time. For Zeenat, Pran, Om Shivpuri, Iftekhar and Shetty, there was no looking back. The music duo of Kalyanji–Anandji was already a big name and *Don* was just a confirmation of what they were capable of. The writers went on to pen the dialogues for more films and, by the time Salim–Javed parted company in the early 1980s, they left behind a legacy that could well be impossible to replicate. Be it the music or the dialogues from *Don,* both have found themselves into mobile phones or just common parlance. To date, Helen still laughs about how she looked so remarkably elegant in 'Yeh Mera Dil'. Can one, for instance, think of the song without the lady? That's not such a difficult one to answer.

Logically, the man who should have gained the most from the unexpected success of *Don* should have been Chandra. A couple of weeks after the film made it big, Manoj called the young and, now successful, director to assist him. Pran happened to be around and when he saw Chandra moving the trolley, his anger knew no limit. In a moment, he grabbed Chandra by his collar and said, 'Do you know who you are? You are Chandra Barot and you have directed *Don.* Stop pushing this trolley now.' The message was clear. Chandra was set for better things and it was time he moved on to make bigger and more successful films. Suddenly, the world around the director looked different. It was clear that he had to emerge from Manoj's shadow.

Ever since *Don* was released, the long queue of producers at Chandra's home was a sight to behold. Over endless cups of tea and generous helpings of food, they would speak of their keenness to sign up the director for forthcoming projects. A rather flattered Chandra was often overwhelmed and, in many moments of privacy, visualized getting bigger over time.

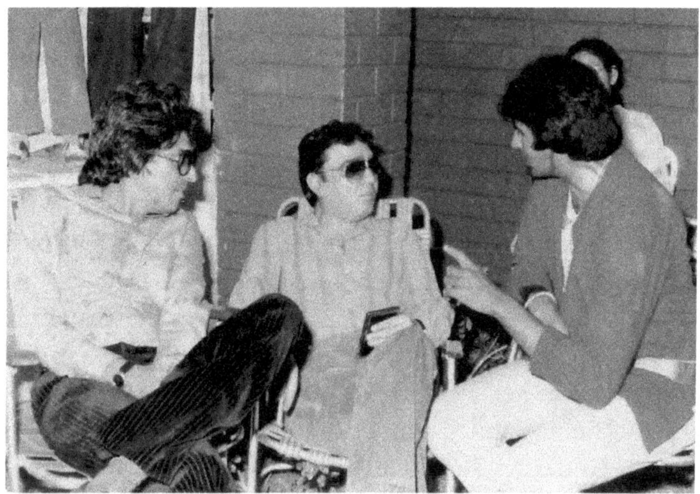

Chandra and Prakash Mehra with Amitabh on the sets of *Coolie* in 1982. This was after his accident

One could not blame him if one had had a debut like *Don*. Unfortunately, destiny took over and the future was not as rosy as it could well have been.

Every project that started was jinxed. A film with Dilip, Manoj, Saira and Anil Kapoor was conceived till someone said it was unviable. The film's financier then felt there would not be too many takers for a film where Dilip would play Manoj's father or, for that matter, how could the audience watch Dilip romancing Saira? The project was shelved. Chandra also started a film with Sarika for which a significant chunk of the shooting was done. In the midst of this, Sarika got into a relationship with Kamal Haasan and nothing came of the film after that.

There was another film titled *Kadi* which had a star cast that included Shashi, Danny Denzongpa, Farah and Rohan Kapur. That ran into some serious financial problems and, eventually, the script was picked up and remade as *Dil* with Aamir Khan and Madhuri Dixit. Of course, *Dil*, a 1990 release directed by Indra Kumar, was a smash hit at the box-office. A project that held some promise was *Lord Krishna* that Sattee Shourie agreed to fund. Chandra signed on twenty-one stars for this very ambitious project. Written by Narendra Sharma, a considerable amount of research also went into it which included sittings with monks just to understand what Krishna was all about. Around that time, Sattee got her daughter, Mona, married to Boney Kapoor. The film took a back seat as Sattee was not comfortable doing such a large project.

Two films planned with Amitabh too never saw the light of day. Understandably, Chandra was distraught and almost convinced that nothing could go right. In 1991, his directorial venture, *Pyar Bhara Dil* was released. Chandra met his wife-to-be, Deepa, on the sets of this film. Not surprisingly, this film has a special place in his heart.

It is not common knowledge that Chandra directed a Bengali film called *Ashrita,* which had a sixty-nine-week run. Starring Mithu Mukherjee, this film was originally started with Dinen Gupta till Chandra was called in to take charge. For the selected few, who have been lucky enough to watch the first few minutes of *Boss,* there is no mistaking the slickness factor that is uniquely Chandra's. The film was started with Vinod but sadly, the star lost interest. Nothing came of it subsequently.

What has not suffered is Chandra's fascination with the visual medium. For decades, he has watched a film every night and the enviable DVD collection is testimony to that. Needless to say, he has every Bond film which he watches over and over again. Today, he spends a lot of time with his son, Akshaan, who is keen on making films.

Chandra still keeps in touch with his close friends from the industry and this includes the likes of Dilip, Saira and Salim, to name a few. He was among the handful of folks who was invited for the Abhishek–Aishwarya wedding. Jaya is still his little sister and the first couple (Amitabh-Jaya) never forgets to wish Chandra on his birthday each year. Theirs is a friendship that goes back to a time that only they know and it was hardly surprising that Jaya came to Chandra's apartment on Peddar Road with her son and Aishwarya just after the couple tied the knot. While it was to greet Chandra and his family, it was also to seek the blessings of his mother. Those in the building were quite taken aback at this high-profile visit which took place without much ado.

Speaking of Amitabh, Chandra, to this day, calls him Tiger. It is a name that a few other close friends address Amitabh by, though Chandra still claims that it was his idea. It was inspired from a Richard Pryor and Gene Wilder film released in the early 1970s. When Chandra and Amitabh watched it in the iconic Eros theatre in Mumbai, the scene where a puny guy is hypnotized and repeatedly called Tiger by the toughie had the audience in splits. Eventually, when the puny one turned around and beats up the burly one, the situation was very comical. For some reason, Chandra saw a resemblance between Amitabh and the poorly built guy on screen. Since then, the name Tiger just stuck. (It was also Amitabh's screen name in *Hum*, a 1991 release).

When Chandra was invited for the premiere of Farhan Akhtar's *Don: The Chase Begins* in 2006, he was somewhat alarmed by the number of interview requests he got from the media. The question everyone asked related to his opinion of the new, remade version. To this day, Chandra says Farhan reached out to an audience that is remarkably different from those who watched the 1978 version. Besides, it was Farhan's way of making a film which deserves to be complimented.

At the premiere, Shah Rukh put away his cigarette when he saw Chandra. Both greeted each other warmly and the young star was very curious about what people said about his performance. Given that Shah Rukh had watched Amitabh in the original, he knew what he was up against. In the end, *Don: The Chase Begins* was the fifth highest grosser of 2006. On a budget of around ₹35 crore, it collected over ₹100 crore globally.

Without a doubt, it was this kind of success that prompted Farhan to make a sequel that he chose to simply call *Don 2*. This much anticipated film was released in the Christmas weekend of 2011. It had already made the news since the satellite and music rights were sold for large sums of money even before the film was released. Produced on a large budget of ₹70 crore, this had Shah Rukh with Priyanka Chopra and Lara Dutta. The film was shot in locations as varied as Malaysia, France, Switzerland and Germany. *Don 2* grossed ₹200 crore at the box-office and was one of the biggest hits of 2011. The last scene of the film has Shah Rukh on his bike that bears a number plate with just *Don 3* written on it. This has led to considerable speculation that there is another sequel that will be made at some point. What thrilled the audience was when Shah Rukh ended *Don 2* with the immortal '*Don ko pakadna mushkil hi nahin, namumkin hai*' line.

Given that there has been such intense debate in the past on how films of an era gone by might have done today, one would do well to take a closer look at the issue. According to ibosnetwork.com, after adjusting for inflation, *Sholay* remains the biggest hit of all time. It places the film's adjusted net collections (taking higher ticket prices and inflation into consideration and deducting entertainment tax) at ₹813.66 crore. Of the biggest hits of the 1970s, *Don* is ranked tenth with a figure of ₹315.32 crore. The corresponding figure for *Don* when it was released stands at ₹7.70 crore. On the performance of the film, ibosnetwork.com calls *Don* an all-time blockbuster that had a golden jubilee run at multiple centres and a platinum jubilee run in Hyderabad.

Three films in the top ten list of the 1970s were released in 1978, with as many as seven of the ten starring Amitabh. Among them are *Sholay*, *Muqaddar ka Sikandar*, *Deewar*, *Trishul* and *Don*. Interestingly enough, films from that era had no revenues coming from the overseas markets. If that had indeed existed, these numbers would be far more impressive.

Did Nariman or Chandra expect *Don* to do as well as it did or, for that matter, did they anticipate that it would be spoken of several years after it was released? Not only is the answer to all this in the negative but it just goes on to prove how the biggest of successes are never planned. That remains the beauty of filmmaking.

To this day, Chandra makes it a point to take the local train in Mumbai to get a feel of what is going on in the city. As it zooms past locations such as the Dhobi Ghat, he gets a little nostalgic about Amitabh running past the washers, who are furiously beating their clothes, with the police hot in pursuit. Yes, it does seem only like yesterday to him. The funny thing is that there is always the passenger on the train who observes Chandra fiddling with the camera. 'Sir, aren't you Chandra Barot?' is the question that inevitably comes up. The last time this took place, Chandra said 'Yes' with a faint smile. The passenger gripped Chandra's hands and said he had watched *Don* five times in 1978. 'You made a film not just for our generation, sir. My teenage son also loves it,' he said. Not bad going at all for a film that was released over three decades ago.

ACKNOWLEDGEMENTS

Writing this book was really the result of a chance meeting with Chandra Barot. I gave this book form and shape over endless cups of tea with him spread over a year coupled with unforgettable stories from Bollywood of the 1970s. In my own mind, this book is really a director's cut and an attempt to narrate Barot's experience of making *Don*.

While writing this book, I was hugely surprised to learn how much the *Don* fan knew about the film. They all have contributed in no small measure to this book. This includes friends from school, college, work and pretty much everywhere, who have taken time out to either watch *Don* again or merely suffer my persistent questioning on the film. A special thank you goes out to my family who probably thought I was more likely to write a book on business.

I am deeply indebted to Chintamani Agashe and Rajesh Ramane, my former colleagues, for their work on the famous *Don* poster. Their understanding of colour and design has never ceased to amaze me.

When the manuscript was initially sent to Rupa Publications India, I was a little unsure about what they would think of a book on the making of a film. Luckily, they liked it and I thoroughly enjoyed working with Pradipta Sarkar and Kadambari Mishra at Rupa.

I hope this book brings back great memories to those who have watched *Don* and tells them something new as well. And just in case you have missed the film, do watch it. It will be worth your while.

ABOUT THE AUTHOR

Krishna Gopalan grew up in Chennai and then Hyderabad, from where he finished his schooling. He acquired a postgraduate degree in Economics from the University of Madras before moving to NMIMS in Mumbai for his MBA. A couple of years in advertising have now been followed by a career in business journalism. He has worked in publications like *The Financial Express*, *Business Today*, *The Economic Times* and *Fortune India* before his current position with *Outlook Business*.

Krishna enjoys films at large, though it was not till the late 1980s that he began watching Hindi cinema in a big way. Over the years, he has managed to catch films across decades, though he believes some of the finest Hindi films were made in the 1970s. Krishna reads widely on subjects like business, films and politics. He lives in Mumbai.

www.ingramcontent.com/pod-product-compliance
Lightning Source LLC
La Vergne TN
LVHW010915110826
845149LV00013B/2373

* 9 7 8 8 1 2 9 1 2 9 1 4 7 *